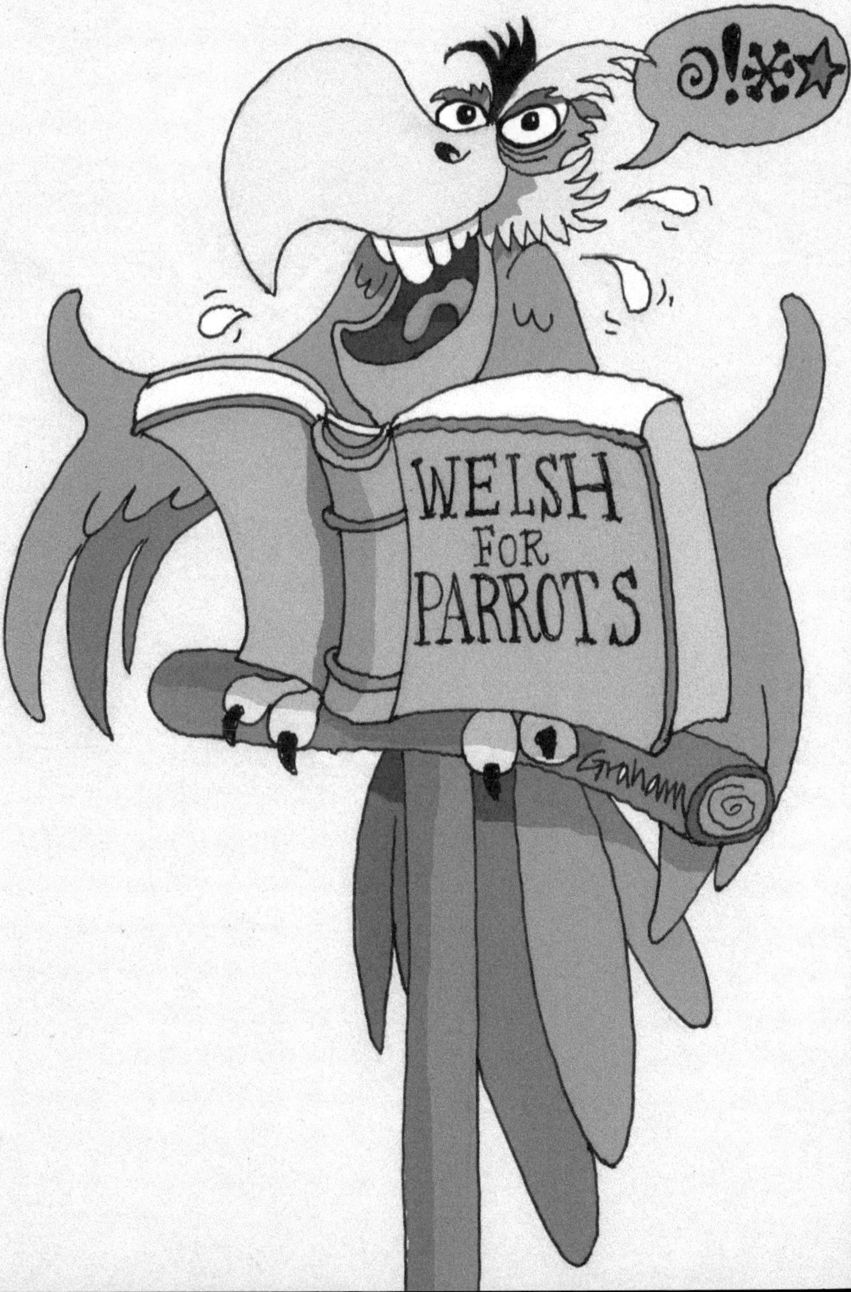
WELSH
FOR
PARROTS
Graham

THE ARTIST:
TALES OF A VERY BLUE PARROT AND OTHER STORIES

IAN MARROW

Copyright © 2016 Ian Marrow

The moral right of the author has been asserted.

Apart from any fair dealing for the purposes of research or private study, or criticism or review, as permitted under the Copyright, Designs and Patents Act 1988, this publication may only be reproduced, stored or transmitted, in any form or by any means, with the prior permission in writing of the publishers, or in the case of reprographic reproduction in accordance with the terms of licences issued by the Copyright Licensing Agency. Enquiries concerning reproduction outside those terms should be sent to the publishers.

This is a work of fiction. Names, characters, businesses, places, events and incidents are either the products of the author's imagination or used in a fictitious manner. Any resemblance to actual persons, living or dead, or actual events is purely coincidental.

Matador
9 Priory Business Park,
Wistow Road, Kibworth Beauchamp,
Leicestershire. LE8 0RX
Tel: 0116 279 2299
Email: books@troubador.co.uk
Web: www.troubador.co.uk/matador
Twitter: @matadorbooks

ISBN 978 1785892 653

British Library Cataloguing in Publication Data.
A catalogue record for this book is available from the British Library.

Printed and bound by CPI Group (UK) Ltd, Croydon, CR0 4YY
Typeset in 11pt Minion Pro by Troubador Publishing Ltd, Leicester, UK

Matador is an imprint of Troubador Publishing Ltd

MIX
Paper from
responsible sources
FSC® C013604

To my family, who doubted my sanity but put up with me while writing this story, and to my friend Julie Rogers, whose move to Bala in Snowdonia first gave me the idea for this work of fiction. Thanks also to my talented pal, cartoonist Richard Graham, who I bribed with wine and food to design the book cover. Lastly, to the people of Bala and its beautiful lake, without whom this would never have been written.

THE ARTIST

Crystal pushed her tangled mop of curly red hair back from her brow and surveyed the mountain of packing cases the removals men had dumped in her new home on the shores of Lake Bala in Wales, before they made a fast escape down the winding road back to Manchester.

"Well, we made it, Perkins." She turned to her pet parrot, sitting in his cage on top of one particularly large stack.

"Bollocks," replied Perkins, followed by a loud wolf whistle.

"Now, Perkins, we have to stop using that language. We're in God-fearing Wales now." Crystal inwardly cursed her ex-boyfriend, and the hours he spent filling the poor bird's head with various curses and obscenities.

"Jolyon is in the past now, Perkins, and you and I are going to learn lovely Welsh words so we fit into our new home. No more bollocks, pillocks and bastards. Do you hear me?"

"Who's a twat?" said Perkins, turning his back, and fluffing up his feathers.

Crystal wiped sweat from her face, and gazed out over the lake. A slight breeze rippled the slate-grey water of Llyn Tegid. She hoped the move would work out. Not much else had in the past three years, ever since she met The Bastard Jolyon. He was past his best even then, and no great shakes in bed – at least not with her. She'd heard rumours about his roving eye, and noticed women friends would avoid sitting next to him. But it was the receipt for the lap-dancing club, found by accident in his suit pocket, that was the last straw. She cut up all his underpants and told him she wanted him and his limp dick out of her life.

Still, the break-up and splitting of assets had, in the end, been more or less amicable, and left her with just enough to buy the quaintly ramshackle cottage overlooking the lake shore, where she now stood contemplating her future.

It was a spur-of-the-moment decision to buy in Wales, taken after she finally removed Jolyon from the Manchester house and planted a 'For Sale' sign outside. Needing a shoulder to cry on she went to Wales for the weekend to visit older sister, Letitia – Tish to everyone who knew her – who lived up the side of a Welsh mountain near Bala, rearing alpacas for their wool.

Crystal poured out her heart to Tish over a couple of bottles of wine. Her sister listened sympathetically, concern showing on her broad weather-beaten face, as Crystal recounted her story. "Mmmm… Mmmm… Bastard… Mmmm… Bastard… What a prick… " intoned Tish between slurps of wine, after each revelation about Jolyon's misdemeanors poured out. Tish drained another large glass of Chablis and helped herself to a refill.

Crystal wiped away a tear. "Anyway, last I heard he was into 'swinging' parties, and going out with some bimbo half his age. Good luck to him – but I hope he gets crabs, or something just as unpleasant, and his fingernails drop out so he can't scratch them.

"You'd think a criminal lawyer would know better, particularly at his age. He wants to be a High Court judge, just like his dad, but I wouldn't be surprised if he didn't end up on the front page of the *Sun* – caught with his pants down in chambers, showing some female juror his briefs.

"For God's sake, Tish, I'm nearly forty years old – too old for this kind of crap. I want to settle down… make something of my life. I'd started to get some decent prices for my paintings – quite a few hundred quid for Nude On A Toadstool. But I've not picked up a paintbrush for months… just can't seem to concentrate and I hate the idea of selling up and living in a rented house again."

It was Tish who came up with the answer. "Come and live in Wales. Seriously, if you can't get inspired here, you can't get inspired anywhere. How about painting Bala Boys In The Buff? In the lake and out. You know, a kind of before and after painting – see how those big boys shrink. Another bottle?"

Both laughed and drank till they were falling off the sofa, but the seed was planted in Crystal's mind and a couple of months later she walked into the local estate agent's on Bala high street, falling for the little stone-built house by the lake the moment she saw the photograph. She couldn't believe how cheap property was in Bala. Even after giving Jolyon his half of the profits from the sale of their terraced house in a fashionable suburb of south Manchester, there was enough money to buy outright.

Now, she looked out over the millpond-still water, the sun setting red at the far end of the lake, and watched as a man in a kayak paddled slowly past. She felt a sense of inner peace absent when she lived in Manchester. "I think it's going to be OK, Perkins."

"Up your arse," replied Perkins.

* * *

Day two and most of Crystal's possessions were stuffed into wardrobes, with the overspill thrown in the attic and piled in the spare room: *I'll worry about that later*, she thought. *Nice day. Time to relax and soak up the last dregs of the summer sunshine.*

Cup of tea in hand and with Perkins' rendition of 'Teenage Dirtbag' ringing in her ears, Crystal stepped into her small front garden. The warmth of the sun kissed her freckled cheeks as she sat, closed her eyes, and listened to the chorus of small birds singing in the trees. She drifted gently off to the avian lullaby. The sun had nearly disappeared when she awakened from her slumber, slightly startled by a man's voice. "Sorry love. Didn't mean to wake you."

Crystal opened her eyes and saw a kind-looking old gent with a walking stick standing by the gate.

"You must be the new owner of Bwythyn Maen Melin." He gestured toward the cottage with his stick. "Lovely lady was renting it before. Pity about that – but welcome to our little community. Huw's the name, by the way."

"Hello Huw. What do you mean, pity?"

"Did no one tell you? Oh dear me. She was trying to throw a dead sheep into the septic tank to get its microbes going again after someone tipped a load of bleach down the drain, and went in herself. There for two weeks she was, before someone noticed a dead sheep in the field, and an awful smell coming from the tank – still open you see. Anyway, they got her body out – the local firemen. Couldn't get the stench off them for a week, I heard. Banned from the local pub they were. Owners decided to sell up after that, but the good news for you is the tank works like a dream now, so they say. Seems her being down there did the trick. Every cloud has a silver lining, eh?"

Crystal looked at her small home, which somehow seemed a little darker, less friendly than before. She shivered, though there was still warmth in the evening air. "Sorry, can I offer you tea or anything?"

"No thank you, my dear. Old man you see. Can't have too many liquids on my walk, or I'd be behind every second tree on my way home. Anyway. Not to worry about the unfortunate accident. What's past is past. How are you settling in? I believe you already have a local connection – the English lady with the strange animals up yonder hill." He vaguely waved his walking stick in the general direction of the steep wooded hillside at the back of the cottage.

"Yes, my sister Tish and her husband live up there. Well, mainly she does. Her husband, George, is away most of the time – works in the City. The animals are alpacas and I'm doing pretty well, thank you." *What a nice old man!*

"In fact, a couple of the alpacas are coming down tomorrow to eat some of my grass in the field next door. Keep it tidy, and it's a free feed for them. I must admit though, I find them a little odd-looking though they are very friendly.

"I'm looking forward to meeting more of the locals like yourself – and hopefully even learn a little Welsh, try to fit into the community."

Huw's eyes brightened, and his wizened face furrowed into a smile. "I can certainly help you there, my dear. Get yourself a pen and paper and I'll get you started with a few useful words and phrases."

Half an hour later, and Crystal waved the old man off. He pottered down the lakeside road into the gathering dusk, muttering something to himself in Welsh, which must have been funny because Crystal caught the sound of laughter as he disappeared from sight. *Good*, she thought. *Something to practice when I go into town shopping. Bore da means good morning. What a fine start.*

* * *

Next day, Tish arrived in her battered old Land Rover, and unloaded two alpacas from the trailer. She herded the animals into the field, and soon they were happily munching on the overgrown grass. Children and parents pointed at the spectacle as the narrow gauge Bala Lake Railway puffed slowly past the cottage, its whistle merrily blowing. Some took snapshots of the strange beasts in the field.

Crystal gazed happily at the bucolic scene and told Tish she was going shopping. "No worries. I'll just settle down and have a cup of tea. Read the papers while you're away," said Tish. "No point in going back home just yet – might as well stay, and then I can take my two big boys back with me. They should have given your little field a good trim by then."

Armed with her list of new Welsh phrases, Crystal strode across the causeway at the bottom end of the lake, where the River Dee begins its journey to the coast. She headed straight into town to Jones the Butcher, hoping all would go well, after practising half the night to try and get a bit of Welshness into her Mancunian accent.

She joined the queue at the door to the shop and eyed the meat on display, deciding a couple of Welsh lamb chops would be just the thing for her evening meal. Finally she reached the head of the queue. "Bore da," she said using the best Welsh accent she could summon. "Ydy pen ol fi yn edrych yn fawr yn hwn?" she intoned from memory.

Mr Jones looked nonplussed, but peered over the counter and said, "Not really, but what can I do for you love?"

Crystal was confused – and her attempt at Welsh met with a similar reaction at every shop she went into – apart from the Co-op, where the assistant listened to her with a blank look on his face, and with a broad Liverpool accent, said, "Sorry missus. I'm from Birkenhead, just helping out with the summer rush. I was told all the locals spoke English."

Maybe I'm just not pronouncing it right, she thought. Still, plenty of time for all that and she had spotted Welsh language courses for beginners at Coleg y Bala. "Trying to run before you can walk again girl," she muttered to herself, as she braced against the strong headwind on the causeway and watched windsurfers take full advantage of the breezy conditions to tack back and forth across the lake.

As she neared her cottage, Crystal noticed the alpacas were no longer in the field. She thought Tish must have gone but no – the Land Rover and trailer were still there. Then she spotted Tish snoozing in the sun, in a chair on the decking at the front. *Maybe they've wandered off.* She quickened her pace toward the house.

Reaching the gate she heard Perkins giving a rendition of one of Jolyon's favourite rugby songs, 'All The Nice Girls Love a Candle'. *Funny, he doesn't usually sing that loud unless he has company. Oh no...* thought Crystal, hurrying into the house. Inside was chaos. Chairs overturned, plates smashed, and two alpacas politely listening to Perkins, who hopped from one leg to another in sheer delight at having such an attentive audience – even if one of them chewed a vintage Moroccan rug while he listened.

"TISH," screamed Crystal, awakening her sister from her siesta. "Your fucking alpacas have wrecked my lounge, and there's shit everywhere. Shoo you fuckin' animals. Out. Out." The beasts seemed reluctant to leave the musical recital, which by now had moved on to 'Alouette', but Tish rushed in and soon had them herded outside, and back into the trailer.

Returning, she found Crystal disconsolately surveying the wreckage, tears in her eyes and clutching what had been a lovely old vase she had years earlier discovered at a French antique market – but which was now in three jagged pieces.

"Sorry. Alpacas are very inquisitive you know – must have heard Perkins and gone to investigate. I just nodded off for a minute," said Tish contritely. "I'd better go. Anyway, the manure is very good for plants, if strained… " Her voice trailed off as she got a hard stare from Crystal and quickly added, "Anyway, must dash. Love you lots and see you soon. Bye."

The cottage door slammed shut behind Tish. "Not a word from you. Not one – or the shit won't be the only thing buried in the garden," Crystal told Perkins as he huffed on his perch.

An hour later, and the lounge was more or less back in place. The rug was beyond repair though. Pity, she reflected. It was bought years ago on a trip to Morocco with her then boyfriend, who spotted it on a street stall in Casablanca. Happy days – they had criss-crossed Europe and North Africa on their journeys in an old camper van, before he got a job working for the United Nations refugee agency in New York, and they drifted apart.

They still kept in touch, with a card at Christmas. He had since married a girl from Brooklyn, and had a growing family of two sons and a daughter – and she had met The Bastard Jolyon. Life could have been so different, she thought, as she remembered his dark good looks, with those intense blue eyes that had so attracted her.

A knock at the door brought Crystal back to the present. *What now?* Perkins perceived he was forgiven, and as Crystal opened the door launched into a particularly rude version of a poem about a ship called Venus and its crew. A rather handsome man stood there, with a large package in his hand. Not bad, she thought. Broad shoulders, slim hips and a nice smile. "Hello." She suppressed the urge to try a welcome in Welsh – that particular experiment didn't seem to have worked so well.

"Noswaith dda," said the young man. "Good evening. I live in the farm about a mile down the road – and just thought I'd pop in and say hello. See if you wanted help with anything. The name's David, by the way."

"That's very kind. Would you like to come in for a minute?" *Farm boy. Won't notice the smell of shit…* she hoped.

"Thank you," said the young man, holding the package toward Crystal. "I brought you some fish. Swimming in the lake half an hour ago it was. Brown trout. About thirty minutes in the oven in a bit of foil with some butter, salt and pepper – go down a treat with a salad and some chips."

"Well thank you, David. Let me just put that in the fridge. I'm about to have a glass of wine. It's been quite a day. Would you like one?"

"Thanks. Red, if you've got it," said David, settling into a battered but comfortable looking armchair, which Crystal had coined 'the chair of truth' since people who sat in it seemed to relax and say what they really meant.

It's certainly the first time a young man has appeared at my door with a gift of fish, thought Crystal, as she poured the wine. *Maybe it's a Welsh thing? Damn sight more practical than flowers, if not quite so traditional.* "There is something you can help me with," she said, as she returned bearing two glasses. "I've been trying very hard to learn some Welsh phrases, but they don't seem to be working very well. I've got them written down somewhere." She fumbled in the drawer in the hall. "Ahh. Here we are," she said, producing the paper on which she had scrawled Huw's phrases.

"Now, let's start with this: 'Ydy pen ol fi yn edrych yn fawr yn hwn?' – am I pronouncing that right?"

David had the same look as the butcher she tried it out on: "Depends what you're trying to say."

Crystal studied the writing. "Well I was told it meant 'Hello, isn't it a beautiful morning?' Have I pronounced it wrong?"

David smiled suddenly – like the sun coming out over the lake, thought Crystal. "You've been speaking to Old Huw, I bet. Walks with a limp, and looks about a hundred years old?"

"That's the one," said Crystal. "He was ever so nice, and very helpful."

David took a quick slurp of his wine, and stifled a smile. "Thing is, Huw's a bit of a joker. Crafty old bugger. Likes to have newcomers on a bit. What you actually said is 'Does my bum look big in this?' He'll be telling everyone at his local, the Glyndwr Arms, about his latest prank, mark my words."

"What about the rest of these phrases?" Crystal blushed for the first time in years, as she handed over the notepaper.

"Let's have a look," said David. "Well this one is 'It's not the men in my life, but the life in my men' and 'I'm not from round here you know'... and 'I want to squeeze your...' I don't think you want to know the rest. It's all a bit... well, colourful."

Crystal was seething. "The old bugger."

"Bugger, bugger, bugger," announced Perkins from the other room.

"What about the previous tenant of this house? He told me she died in a tragic accident. Fell into the septic tank."

"No. She's still very much alive. Went to Wrexham to be near her daughter and grand-children. I don't think Old Huw means any real harm – just can't stop himself, and has a bit of a hard time accepting all the new people who are arriving. Anyway, is that the time? Must dash," said David, glancing at his watch and draining his glass. "Farm doesn't look after itself unfortunately."

After David left, Crystal still seethed, and decided Old Huw wasn't going to get away with making her a laughing stock. A notion began to gather shape in a corner of her mind – until at last she had a plan of action. "He's picked the wrong one, Perkins. I might cry – but then I get even."

"Kick him in the goolies," suggested Perkins helpfully.

"Oh no," she told him, tickling under his beak. "I've got something far better in mind – more on the lines of an eye for an eye…"

* * *

Crystal delved into as yet unopened packing cases, and unearthed her paints, brushes, and all the other components of her profession, to start work on the revenge: *Try and make a fool of me would you eh, Old Huw?* The Bastard Jolyon had taken the piss… Old Huw had taken the piss. *Now it's my turn!*

She set up her easel, found a decent canvas and set to work, feeling inspired as the painting took shape. Painting Huw's face from memory – she had never had a problem with almost total recall – she began building the picture. Every brush stroke meticulous as the image built, and her imagination took flight. Finally, after burning the midnight oil for two nights, she sat back satisfied. The painting was complete.

The next day she wrapped it in a large tea towel, and set off across the causeway in search of the Glyndwr Arms. It took a while to find the pub – at the back of the main street, down a small alleyway. A single flickering light illuminating a dingy sign told Crystal she had arrived at the infamous Glyndwr Arms. Tish had told her it was a hotbed of Welsh nationalism, and not a place to visit if you fancied a friendly evening down at the pub. It was late morning, and surveying the room she saw it must be a quiet time for the licensed trade in Bala. Two men sat on stools, cradling pints of beer in their hands, and a large tattooed man stood behind the bar, his belly protruding from the bottom of a tee shirt emblazoned with a Welsh dragon. She was aware of the sudden silence as three pairs of eyes followed her as she walked in.

Take a deep breath – shoulders back girl, best foot forward, as Brown Owl always said. She marched to the bar. "Sorry, I'm English. Don't speak Welsh, but I'm going to learn. I have a present for you."

With a flourish she removed the tea towel, and listened with satisfaction to the collective gasp from three open mouths. "Pity Huw isn't here. After all this is dedicated to him. You may have heard of me. I'm the new woman in the cottage by the lake, who says funny things when she tries to speak Welsh, Huw-style. I'm sure he's told you all about me." Their reaction and failure to meet her gaze confirmed that Huw had indeed regaled the regulars about his little joke at her expense.

The four of them regarded the painting, and Crystal had to say it was one of the best nudes she had painted. She admired the meticulous detail of Old Huw, naked as the day he was born – every wrinkle and crease on display. He was standing in a field along with a flock of Welsh mountain sheep who looked very worried. About the only thing that wasn't wrinkled about Huw was his appendage, which hung out from his body and was clearly the principal cause of the flock's alarm.

"I would be very grateful if you could hang this in pride of place behind the bar. I'm sure Huw would appreciate it – he likes a joke, as you all know."

The landlord looked unsurely at the painting. "I don't know love. I have my licence to consider, and some may think it's a bit, you know, near the knuckle if you get my meaning."

But Crystal stood her ground. "I'm a well-established artist with a good reputation, and I can assure you this is bona fide art. I'm offering it to you for nothing – apart from a promise that it will hang in pride of place behind your bar, in perpetuity. Who knows? Could be worth a fortune one day."

The landlord still looked a bit worried, but one of the regulars piped up, "Come on, Taff. Huw's always taking the piss – time someone got their own back for a change. Go on boy."

"Can't wait to see Huw's face when he sees this," said the other.

And they both cheered as Taff accepted the picture, propping it up by the optics. "I'll hang it up properly later – I promise. In the meantime I insist on buying you a pint. Took some nerve coming in here, and I must admit you've got Huw off to a tee. Certainly his face. Wouldn't like to say about the rest."

"I'd be delighted to accept," said Crystal, levering herself onto a stool between the two lunchtime drinkers. "A pint of Brains bitter and crisps all round, Taff. I hate drinking on an empty stomach."

* * *

The effect of Crystal's painting was remarkable. She was no longer a stranger on the streets of Bala – and the time taken on shopping trips had doubled as people stopped her in the streets to chat, and praise her for stuffing it to Old Huw. She found many others had suffered at his hands over the years – and wanted to meet the woman who had finally managed to get even. "Made a proper fool of him, you did, and good on you. It's the talk of Bala. Time someone gave him a taste of his own medicine," was the typical reaction.

"Started a rumour I was pregnant – truth is I like doughnuts a bit too much," one slightly plump young woman told her as they queued in the Co-op. "It got back to my boyfriend – and he knew it couldn't be him. Very careful he was. So that was that – finished. I cried for a week. I really liked that boy too. Never forgave that old bastard."

Crystal's growing reputation meant she started to get commissions locally. "If I give you a photograph can you paint my husband? Nothing too racy, and definitely no sheep, but he's coming up sixty years old and I want something special to surprise him," was one request. "And if it's not asking too much, can you sort of… elongate him? He's a bit sensitive, see. Not a lot showing till he gets interested."

Crystal laughed. "My pictures do tend to accentuate the positive. I promise you he'll be happy with the result, and so will you." Then one day, the inevitable happened – staggering out of the Spar shop with two heavy bags of shopping, Crystal almost collided with Old Huw who was shuffling down the pavement in the direction of the White Lion. She stared him up and down defiantly. "Hello, Huw," she said finally. "I believe you've been keeping a bit of a low profile. Been to the Glyndwr Arms recently? I go there quite a lot nowadays – and very popular I am, for a silly little English woman in a Welsh pub."

Old Huw smiled, a little sadly she thought. "I have changed my drinking habits somewhat. Sorry if my little joke offended. I just can't help myself sometimes. Any chance we can call a truce? Let bygones be bygones."

Crystal dumped her shopping on the pavement and contemplated, pausing for a full ten seconds. "Trouble is, Huw, it's not just me. I've been listening to people – lots of them – and I have to say mostly women. I think you really have a problem. I forgive you – I really do. And in some ways you've done me a favour, because if there was a way to get known in Bala you've certainly helped me to do it. But what about everyone else? Some horrible stories. It's got to stop. Do you hear me?"

Huw shuffled uncomfortably on the pavement. "I'll try," he said. "Started years ago after my wife died, and I was left alone. Nothing to do, you see, and you know what they say – the Devil makes work for idle hands. Must admit though, I enjoyed it, and had a right laugh over the years. But I've seen the error of my ways. Promise."

Crystal felt a little sorry for him, but suddenly had a thought. "Is this all true, Huw? Or am I going to hear that your wife is alive and well and waiting for you at home with your dinner on the table?"

"No, it's true – honestly," said a shamefaced Huw.

"Tell you what," said Crystal. "I'll give you something to do. Teach me Welsh – properly this time or there could well be another painting. You have no idea how creative I can be. And maybe we can be friends. Deal?" she asked holding out her hand.

"Mae'n llawer," said Huw, accepting her shake. "I'll tell you what that means over a cup of tea if you have your purse open?"

"Don't push it Huw. You're buying, and I'll have a rather large glass of white wine, thank you."

* * *

Three months later and lots of new friends had arrived in Crystal's life. There was Sylvie who lived in a remote farmhouse at the top of the hill – just a few feet short of a mountain, she had told Crystal –and Ted, the local farmer who kept sheep in one of her fields at the back of the cottage. There were many more she now knew on nodding terms when she went shopping on the high street. But she particularly looked forward to visits from David – and had grown fond of the big farmer and his cheerful smile, finding him straightforward and honest. A lot cleverer than he let on as well, she had found out, when he mentioned in passing that he had a first-class degree in agricultural management. Looking out of her front window she saw him arriving at the gate – rather more smartly dressed than usual and carrying a bunch of flowers.

Crystal opened the door before he had chance to knock. "Hello David. No fish today?"

"No. Flowers, now that I've come courting, since you have kindly agreed to come out with me."

Crystal's brow furrowed. "I like you a lot, David, but… I don't recall ever saying I'd go out with you. I'm sure I'd remember that."

"But you accepted the fish," said David. "It's tradition round here: I ate the trout – you can take me out."

"Well… I… um," began Crystal, before noticing the smile growing on David's face.

"We all like a bit of a joke here in Bala, you know. Sorry, I couldn't resist. But how about it? I know you didn't have much of a time with the last chap in your life, but I like to think I could do a bit better – and when the fish are out of season, I have lamb in my freezer, and a farmyard full of chickens."

"Well, in that case you'd better come in," said Crystal. "And if we get really hungry there's scraggy old parrot ripe for the oven."

"Ti'n Goc Oen," Perkins piped up from the other room.

BALA HAS TALENT

Crystal nursed a cup of tea and watched from her window as the last of the autumn leaves blew like rain-sodden confetti from trees outside the cottage. The remnants of Hurricane Harry had arrived in North Wales after crossing the Atlantic from Bermuda, and a fierce wind whipped up the waters of Llyn Tegid. White peaks topped the waves that ran across the lake and crashed against rocks lining the causeway, drenching anyone foolhardy enough to try and walk along the road.

From the upstairs windows of the cottage she could see that flooding had caused the River Dee to burst its banks in several places, turning fields into large ponds that had already become temporary homes for ducks, seagulls and even a stately swan. A lone windsurfer sped across the lake's stormy water.

"Look at that daft bugger! Nice and cosy in here though isn't it Perkins?" She turned from the bleak scene outside the window. Perkins squawked loudly, which she took to be agreement. "Only eight weeks to Christmas. I just hope the cottage survives the storm intact. First big test of winter weath—"

A large crash, and a flash that lit up the lane outside, interrupted her and she gasped in surprise as a wooden electricity pylon fell to the ground in a tangle of sparks and wires. The cottage lights flickered, and died, leaving Crystal and Perkins in eerie semi-darkness. The TV stopped and the cottage was oddly quiet, as background noises from Homes Under The Hammer and the hum of electrical appliances was silenced. For once even Perkins was speechless, hiding his head under a wing.

"Don't worry, Perkins. I'm sure they'll soon come and fix it – I've got my old camping equipment somewhere." Crystal tried to picture where it might be in the jumble of belongings still piled high in the spare bedroom and the attic. "A torch. That's what I need. And I'll bring some wood inside for the log burning stove. We don't really need all these new-fangled things like central heating, electricity and fridges do we Perkins?… shit, the freezer's full of lamb from David's farm. Better ring him on the mobile… bugger the old days."

Crystal punched buttons on her iPhone. "Hello, Mrs Owen. Sorry to trouble you, but there's a pylon down in the lane and the electricity's off. I wondered if David could spare a moment? Yours is off too – oh dear… do you want me to ring back? OK. Thanks. I'll wait, if you really don't mind."

Sounded a bit grumpy, thought Crystal. She probably just has a lot on her plate with the electricity being down, but she had noticed Mrs Owen never seemed very cheerful or friendly during their short conversations.

She heard Mrs Owen's footsteps cross the flagged floor of the farmhouse kitchen to the door, and her shout across the yard, "Dafydd. Mae Crystal ar y ffôn." Several minutes passed before Crystal heard the door open and slam shut, and footsteps approach the phone.

"Hello, David. I know you must be busy, but as I was just telling your mum, the electricity's off and all this lamb in the freezer is going to start defrosting if it's not back on soon. How are you doing up at the farm? Your mum said you were off as well."

"We're OK," said David. "Working farm, you see, so we have a generator. We're used to this happening in winter. Last time there was a storm like this, the electricity was off for nearly a fortnight. Absolute chaos, and electricity cables down all over Wales, so I wouldn't be expecting miracles. You could come and stay here for a while. Spare room, mind. Mum's a bit traditional you know."

"We'll be all right," said Crystal, picturing uncomfortable silences. She suspected Mrs Owen didn't approve of her, and certainly wouldn't take kindly to Perkins' sometimes colourful language. "We have the log burner, and a camping kettle somewhere. Suppose I should have guessed there might be problems when I found a big box of candles left by the last tenant in the cupboard under the stairs."

"I'll come over when I have a minute, pick up the lamb, and see you're OK. I've got some lamps and I'm sure I have a kettle if you can't find yours. The gas hob'll still be working, as long as you have something to light it with, so at least you'll be able to make a cup of tea and live on food from the top of the stove for a bit. Look, I'll be over as soon as I can, but you can imagine, we're pretty busy at the moment."

Crystal put the phone down and shivered – even though the temperature in the lakeside cottage hadn't yet started to drop. "Welcome to winter in North Wales, Perkins. Just have to make do – tell you what, let's play a game – you be Bob Cratchit and I'll be Scrooge, sitting with scratchy pens in our unheated home, with candles making big reflections on the wall."

"Cobblers," said Perkins, shuffling on his perch – his composure now recovered.

"Suit yourself, killjoy."

* * *

David was proved right, and days later the electricity hadn't been restored. The local radio news informed Crystal that engineers were working flat out to mend broken connections across North and Mid Wales, but with no timetable for when the electricity would be back on. She almost began to enjoy the new simple life. There was no television to distract her, and the log burning stove cast a merry glow over the living room walls – bit cold in the bedroom, though, even in her fluffy Beauty and the Beast jim jams and with an extra duvet on the bed. "This is all getting me in the spirit of Christmas, Perkins, but if they don't get a move on we'll be cooking the turkey on the barbecue outside, or in bits in a frying pan. Tish is in the same boat as us, but at least she can go and live in the yurt outside the farmhouse if it gets too cold."

Tish told her the yurt, put up in a clearing in the wood for holiday lets, was warm in the coldest weather, even if it was a bit smoky with the wind in the wrong direction. "Best thing I ever bought," Tish told her. She had spotted the Mongolian tent-like structure on the YurtsRUs website. "Didn't even need planning permission as it's not classed as a permanent structure, and the grockles love it. What with the alpacas roaming round as well, we look quite ethnic. Bit mixed up, since they're from South America, but most people wouldn't know an alpaca from a yak if they fell over one, so we just keep shtum."

She offered Crystal use of the yurt, but Crystal said she would rather stay in the cottage. It was only a little over a mile into Bala town, and she could go and get warm, check her emails and charge up her laptop at the internet café on the high street. The farmhouse was miles from anywhere up a narrow, rough track, which Crystal's little Honda Jazz found hard going – particularly in winter, with snow and ice on the road. The last time she had attempted the road in bad conditions, the car had slipped backwards into a gorse bush, and had to be towed free by a local farmer with his Land Rover. Her little car still carried the battle scars, and she didn't want a repeat performance.

The sound of letters dropping through the postbox jolted Crystal from her reverie, and when she peered through the window, Wayne, the postie, gave her a cheery wave. Crystal waved back, and smiled as she remembered Wayne's recent visit as a client. Soon to retire after more than forty years pushing letters through boxes in Bala and surrounding areas, he had commissioned her to paint a picture of him, to send out as cards for his leaving do at the Glyndwr Arms.

Candlelight had cast strange shadows on the old postie's

naked form as Crystal worked her magic – including the signature 'enhancement' which most of her male clients requested – and gave the painting an almost 3-D effect.

The finished result showed Wayne, naked apart from an old-fashioned postman's hat and sack, outside a house with parcels and letters in both hands and a puzzled look on his face as he pondered how to announce his presence. Underneath was the legend: 'THE POSTMAN ALWAYS KNOCKS TWICE: BUT WAYNE GOES HANDS-FREE.'

She sifted through the letters he had left on her doormat – mostly junk mail – but also a letter from best pal Freddie in Manchester, the address written in characteristic looping handwriting, with a smiley face after Crystal's name. *I'll read that with a cup of tea later*, she thought. Looking through the rest of the pile she found two gems in the general litter of leaflets. With an audible sigh of expectation, she immediately opened the 'Presents for Christmas' catalogue from Santas-sack.com. Such wonderfully silly gift ideas – a large thermal sock that fitted both feet for relaxing in front of the fire; a 6-foot tall inflatable Santa for the garden; a set of musical nappies that played a merry Christmas tune when wet (suitable for all ages); a nose-hair strimmer; a full-face turkey hat and a pine tree-shaped stopper to re-seal a bottle of wine once opened – *certainly won't need that one. And that was just page one. David's Christmas stocking is going to be really daft this year*, she thought, setting the booklet aside for more detailed research later.

There was also a leaflet that looked like it had been printed from a home computer, advertising the annual Bala Has Talent charity show at the old cinema on the high street the week before Christmas – all proceeds to Children In Need. Contestants needed. The first prize was a candlelit dinner for two at the Plas-Yn-Dre restaurant in the town centre and £100 worth of Co-op vouchers. *Now that's an idea*, she thought. *What could David and I do? A Laurel and Hardy double act… no that's no good – it would mean coming up with a workable script, and who would play the fat one?* David would insist it be her. Then Crystal remembered when she and Freddie had wowed all their friends with a rendition of Sonny and Cher's 'I've Got You Babe', at a fancy dress wig party in Manchester – even if The Bastard Jolyon had unkindly suggested someone put the cats out. "What do you think, Perkins? Would David and I be any good?"

Perkins regarded her with a beady eye, but said nothing.

"I'll take that as a yes. Now all I have to do is persuade David out of his 'I'm a strong and silent farmer' mode, and find his inner self as a long-haired singer from the 1960s, who – let's face it – to our modern eyes looked like a bit of a twat. Just need some sheepskin to make into sleeveless jackets, a couple of wigs, and we're off. If you feel left out, we can always get you a mini-wig and jacket. How would that be my little Perky Werky?" she said, tickling him under his beak. He made a half-hearted attempt to nip her finger, but Crystal laughed and pulled her hand away.

* * *

That night in bed, Crystal cuddled up close to David, her index finger casually tracing circles on his chest. "David?" She felt him tense. *Bugger. He was getting to know her too well.*

"What? Whatever it is the answer's probably going to be no," he said, defensively snuggling deeper into the duvet until only his eyes and the top of his head were visible..

"You know you like charity work, helping kids – that kind of thing?"

"I do my bit when I can," he replied – caution in every word and body signal. "Ran the three peaks last year in a sponsored race, and this year I took part in the Young Farmers' sheep shearing contest. Even came close to beating Myfanwy – would have but she had a more docile sheep than me. They were both for charity, and I think they raised quite a bit. That the sort of thing you were thinking about?"

"Something a bit like that, but not anything nearly as

strenuous, and something we could do together. Please, David. Please, say you'll help. Mr Willy thinks I can make it worth your while." Crystal slipped her hands under the sheets. "My my, someone's already standing to attention, ready to volunteer." *Sometimes this was just too easy.*

"The Welsh are great singers, and all you'd have to do is join me in a song and dress up a bit – what could be easier?"

"What song? And what sort of dress? I'm not being a woman, and that's flat. No matter what you do. Ooooo – stop. OK, tell me the worst – what is it?"

Crystal produced the leaflet from where she had put it, upside down, on the bedroom table, and watched as David read it. "Sonny and Cher – remember them from the old Top of the Pops re-runs? I think we'd be great. We might even win. You've gone very quiet, David. Speak to me."

David turned in the bed. "Thank God for that. I thought I was going to have to be a Pussy Cat Doll or something. You know what they say – In for a penny, in for a pound. Let's do it."

Crystal shrieked with delight. "There are times, David, when you surprise even me. Come on, give me a hug you big softie."

* * *

The next day Crystal downloaded a 1965 version of 'I Got You Babe' from YouTube onto her laptop, and began to practice, singing along to Cher's vocals and trying to copy her mannerisms. Bit shaky on the top notes, she thought, but plenty of time before the show. "God, I wasn't even born when this was made, Perkins. Hard to think it was fifty years ago. You not joining in? I know you prefer something a bit raunchier, but come on. Give me the old Perkins perch shuffle." Crystal wiggled her hips to the music. Perkins regarded her with a cold beady-eyed stare, and a grumpy shake of his head.

"Killjoy. Get into the spirit, Perkins – it's nearly Christmas, and we already have the candlelight – just need the crackers and the turkey, and a bottle or two of wine… "

The practice session was interrupted by a knock at the door – Old Huw standing there cupping his hand to his ear.

. "Come in Huw. I'll put the kettle on. Any reason for the visit, or just popping in for a chat?"

"No reason," said Huw. "I was just passing, and heard what I thought sounded like someone was in pain. Are you OK?"

"That was me singing, Huw. Cheeky bugger. Perkins and I thought it was lovely. Didn't we Perkins? Well, I did anyway. I was practising for the Bala Has Talent competition just before Christmas."

"Funny you should say that. I've entered too," said Huw. "I'm doing my celebrated version of the classic 'Keep Right On To The End Of The Road', but in my native Welsh language and dressed like the great Harry Lauder – crooked walking stick and all. First performed for Opportunity Knocks In Bala in 1966 and in competitions every year since. I have great hopes for a win this time – fiftieth time lucky."

Crystal pondered whether she was stating the bleedin' obvious. "Sounds interesting Huw, but you do realise that Harry Lauder was Scottish?"

"That's it. Exactly. Got it in one," exclaimed Huw excitedly, his rheumy eyes glowing with enthusiasm. "It's a sort of Gaelic/Cymric crossover, if you see what I mean. Leaves people wondering – makes them think a bit."

Think, and wonder whether the daft old git's lost all his marbles, thought Crystal – but said nothing. *If this is the strength of the competition, David and I have it in the bag – I can almost taste the fillet steak.*

"Any word yet on when the electricity's going to be on, Huw?" asked Crystal from the kitchen, as she poured boiling water into what had once been her mother's stained old teapot, and reached for the tin of home-made bara brith.

"Still not got past repairing the downed lines in Dolgellau, I heard," said Huw. "Fellow in the Glyndwr Arms last night reckons it could be another two weeks before they get to these parts – and he's one of the men working on the line, so he should know. He'd had a few, mind, but it was the worst storm in twenty years for damage, he reckoned. Should be back on before Christmas though, with a bit of luck."

"That's reassuring," said Crystal. "Let's just hope we don't have another little puff of wind, or a flake of snow falling between now and then."

Huw sipped his tea, and wrapped his dentures round a slice of bara brith. "In the country now, Crystal love. Things happen a bit more slowly here. Rest of our lives to live – no point in worrying about little things like a bit of electricity."

"Need to get some extra staff in – a few Poles up those poles, if you know what I mean. Be fixed in a week. Rural life is one thing – I want my leccy back. Go, go, go," said Crystal in her best Welsh accent, poking Huw in the ribs. "Anyway, how about giving me a bit of Harry in Welsh?"

Huw put his cup of tea down, cleared his throat and sang, his voice filling the tiny kitchen – not exactly Land of My Fathers, but not bad Crystal had to admit.

On the other side of the room Perkins joined in – bloody traitorous bird. "Have a bit of bara brith, Perkins. I hope it bloody chokes you," she muttered under her breath.

* * *

The day of the competition drew near, and David was finally persuaded to take it seriously, and join her for an hour's dress rehearsal, before leaving to muck out a cow shed or something, Crystal supposed. Sheepskin jackets, crafted from an old no-longer fashionable rug, wigs borrowed from the dress shop on the high street and two pairs of bell-bottomed jeans she had found online completed the ensemble. Crystal thought David looked more like a rugby player in drag than Sonny, but kept quiet in case it put him off – anyway, it added a comic touch to the performance, she decided.

But for now the show had to take a back seat to work – it seemed the must-have Christmas present this year in Wales was a nude painting, and today her clients included an elderly couple of keen walkers. *Beats a selfie in silly hats with tongues hanging out*, thought Crystal, as she consulted her diary. Maybe she would have to get a waiting room if it got much busier, draft Perkins in as receptionist. "The artist in residence will see you now. Just leave your clothes on the chair when you go in," she imagined Perkins being trained to say, though he'd have to drop his customary "bollocks" at the end of the sentence.

Seen more genitalia than the local doctor this month, she pondered. All shapes, sizes and ages had paraded through her little studio – now moved from the unheated studio-cum-shed to the front room until the electricity was back on. The couple, naturists from Llandudno, were two lovely old ducks – but had given Crystal quite a task, coping with the nuances of their wrinkly torsos. Like a couple of Shar Peis, she thought, as she posed them before the backdrop they had asked for – a picture of the towering crevices of Cader Idris. Complete with walking sticks, their tanned but droopy faces were poised over a map, as if planning their ascent of the mountain that towered over the market town of Dolgellau. It was a rather surreal scene, thought Crystal, as she laboured over the canvas to catch every crevice – on both mountain and subjects. It put her in mind of one of her favourite Lake District walks, Crinkle Crag. She smiled as she painted – bit of finishing off needed, but the preliminaries were almost done. The rest she could complete from memory. "I'll have this ready for you in about a week – just need to paint in some of the backdrop and finish off some of the finer details."

"That's fine. We'll call round and pick it up. It'll be hanging over the mantelpiece in time for Christmas dinner with all our friends," said the woman.

Crystal pictured the couple and their friends all sitting

down to a naturist Christmas meal – only the turkey arriving at table with dressing. "You must come walking with us one day," said the man. "I saw when we came in that you had a decent set of boots by the door, and I'm sure you'd enjoy it. From here we could go on the little railway to Llanuwchllyn, and walk from there to the summit of Aran Benllyn – it's about 10 miles of pretty rough scrambling, but the scenery along the way is spectacular with views of several mountain ranges, and looking back is Llyn Tegid. On a clear day I believe you can see all the way to Ireland – not that there's many of those. What do you think?"

Both looked expectantly at Crystal, who thought she'd have to choose a particularly cold day, so everyone would be forced to dress up warm. She conjured up an image of them striding across a bleak landscape with no clothes on, everything swinging apart from the old fellow's todger – shrunk to nothing in the cold. "That would be nice, but I'm pretty busy at the moment – what with work, and rehearsing for Bala's Got Talent the week before Christmas. I haven't even thought about what I'm doing on Christmas Day yet." Crystal immediately regretted what she had just said.

"You must come to us," announced the woman. "We only live just up the coast, and you can bring a friend if you want – stay the night, so you don't have to drive. It would be lovely to see you, and you can meet all our friends – I'm sure some of them will want paintings too."

"I'll have to talk to David, see what he wants to do," said Crystal diplomatically, sure it wouldn't be eating his turkey in the buff with a load of old wrinklies.

She was relieved when they finally started clambering into clothes to make their exit – at least they wouldn't scare the sheep, who were munching grass in the field next to the house, on their way to their car.

* * *

The day before the show, and Crystal woke up with the feeling something was different, but couldn't quite work out what, as she lay snuggled under piled-up duvets. Then she had it – it was warm. In the background she heard the faint metallic click of a radiator warming up. The electricity must have come back on, and automatically fired up the boiler.

She felt slightly sad that the adventure was over – her days making do without the usual home comforts finished – but was still relieved when she tried her bedside lamp and found it worked. "Perkins," she shouted. "As they would say at Houston space centre – we have lift off. And it's my special day to watch Homes Under The Hammer."

Nearly nine o'clock, she thought, as she clambered out of bed. *Getting lazy. Must be country living.* In Manchester the traffic always woke her as the rush hour got underway, and she rarely slept past 7am. Here, there was no noise apart from birdsong and sheep. Crystal found that now she sometimes slumbered on if she forgot to set the alarm and the dawn chorus didn't wake her.

"Lot to do today, Perkins," said Crystal, as she walked to the kitchen. "Everything that's been keeping cool outside needs to go back into the fridge, and I have to finish off that painting. Droopy and his mate will be back today to pick it up, and I need to do a final practice for the show tomorrow night. David's coming over later, so I need to go into Bala and get something to eat – and stock up the fridge again while I'm at it."

Crystal had been living hand-to-mouth for the past couple of weeks and realised she would soon have to think about Christmas. The letter from Freddie, inviting her to spend Christmas with her and Nigel in Manchester was still on the mantelpiece. They lived in a luxury apartment near the top of Beetham Tower, Manchester's tallest building and one of the highest residential developments in Europe, with sweeping views over the Cheshire Plains. But Crystal thought she would prefer to spend it in Bala. She knew David wouldn't be able to get away for Christmas, unless he had his widowed mum in tow, and as a traditional Welsh country woman, Mrs Owen would be decidedly frosty in the company of Freddie – loud even by Manchester standards.

Freddie's usual Christmas cast-list of waifs and strays from the far corners of the city's louche set were also a virtual guarantee of disharmony – she even doubted if David would be able to get along with them, never mind his mother. Mrs Owen already seemed to regard Crystal as dangerously bohemian, but just about tolerated her for the sake of her son. Crystal recalled telling her of their plans to impersonate Sonny and Cher at Bala's Got Talent, and got the look that said "Why would I be surprised, dear?"

No, it would probably be lunch at home, and maybe after that she and David would hopefully have a little time together. "That'll be nice, won't it Perkins?"

"Can it, schmuck," said Perkins in perfect imitation of a New York accent.

Crystal had put the television on for background noise, and saw that an old James Cagney film was playing on the movie channel. "I think life was definitely better before the electricity went back on," she said.

"Eat lead, sister," said Perkins.

*　*　*

The day of the competition finally dawned, and as Crystal enjoyed her early morning cuppa in bed she saw through her window that the high winds and rain had returned. Waves again swept along the lake, and the reed beds on the shore had disappeared underwater as rivers and streams that fed Llyn Tegid swelled the lake, and again filled the River Dee almost to overflowing. Fir trees outside the cottage whipped around like they were in the midst of a tropical storm and the wind's melancholy howl sounded like the agonised cry of a huge beast. Crystal hoped this didn't mean another spell without electricity, and she touched the wooden table at the side of her bed in a superstitious good luck gesture.

She and David had practised the song together, and she was pretty sure they could remember all the words – which were not exactly complicated. She had the soundtrack to sing along to and the lyrics written down. They'd be all right, touch wood, but she might need to hug one of the bloody trees outside for the magic to really work if David didn't buck up his ideas, thought Crystal.

She had a bottle of champagne in the fridge in case they won, and a much cheaper bottle of Spanish Cava, picked up on the last visit to Aldi in Wrexham, if they lost – in which case the champagne could wait till Christmas.

Crystal quickly dressed, and sat at her workbench, to put the finishing flourishes to several commissioned works. The naturist couple called to collect their painting. She was relieved when they didn't repeat their invitation to spend Christmas with them, and was surprised when she went to the door to wave them goodbye, to find it was already getting dark. She glanced at the wall clock and it was 3.30pm, time for a quick snack and to start getting ready for the competition.

Where had the day gone? David was due in an hour, and the competition started at 7pm.

Crystal stepped into the shower, luxuriating in the spray of hot water that splashed over her body. "Thank you, God of electricity. Long may you be with us."

Finished, she towelled down, and walked into the spare room where her outfit was laid on the bed alongside David's. Quickly changing, Crystal tied her unruly red locks into a tight bun and completed the transformation into Cher with the long black wig. She was applying lots of black mascara to her eyes when she heard David's pick-up in the drive.

The door opened, and she heard David's welcoming call: "Hello. Where are you?"

"I'm up here," shouted Crystal in reply. "Come up. I've got your costume ready."

She heard footsteps on the stairs, and David appeared. "What do you think?" Crystal treated David to a pirouette.

"Sure you'll look better than I do," said David noncommittally as he struggled into his bell-bottomed jeans, to which Crystal had added large ornamental metal buttons down each outside seam. "Must have put a few pounds on since you bought these. I'm sure they fitted better last time," said David, struggling with the top button.

Crystal noticed that, indeed, David's belly was hanging over the jeans – crash diet for you, after Christmas, she decided, but said, "You look fine. Get the wig on and we're done. Just time for a quick pint at the Glyndwr Arms – bit of Dutch courage before the show."

"You're surely not suggesting we go in dressed like this," said David, regarding himself in the full-length mirror.

"It'll be fine. Who's going to recognise you?" said Crystal. "Come on – live a little, and stop looking like you're going to a funeral."

The Glyndwr Arms was packed when Crystal and David walked in. Johnny Cash had lined up pints of lager on the bar, and his companion Dolly Parton downed a pint of Rosie's Scrumpy cider. Elsewhere, Crystal noticed what looked like a very spotty version of One Direction, and Elvis was leaving the room – heading in the direction of the lavvy. Old Huw turned and waved. He was dressed in a kilt nearly down to his ankles and held a walking stick made from what looked like a sturdy piece of corkscrew willow. "Hello, looks like we have a couple of hippies here," he greeted. "Up from Glastonbury for the day in the VW campervan, are we?"

"Pot and kettle, eh Huw? You look like a hobbit version of Braveheart without the blue face. Bilbo MacBaggins. Mine's a pint of Brains bitter, and David will have the same."

She glanced round the pub. "Quite a crowd in here tonight, and most look like they're here for the show judging by some of the get-ups."

Hugh scanned the bar, while he scrabbled in his sporran for his purse. The landlord Taff was already pulling two pints. "What is it?" He peered over the bar at their outfits. "Mick Jagger and Keith Richards?"

"Cheeky bugger," said Crystal. "Don't you recognise Sonny and Cher when you see them?"

Taff looked them up and down. "No. Can't see it myself. Could be Max Wall and Tommy Trinder in drag though – that'd be worth watching."

"Ho ho ho. Very funny. You won't be laughing when we're heading off for a steak dinner with £100 of Co-op vouchers in our back pockets," said Crystal, quickly slurping back her pint. She noticed the bar was rapidly emptying. "Come on David. Show time."

* * *

Crystal and David entered the old cinema by a back door, which had a large placard with an arrow and the single word 'Contestants' written on it. The ancient heating system had been cranked up, and at least it was warm. Crystal peered through the stage curtains, and saw the auditorium was filling with people – many of whom she recognised, but there were also quite a few unfamiliar faces.

Turning, she saw the contestants, who had earlier been taking a pint or two in the Glyndwr Arms, limbering up for the show. Old Huw had dug out a small flask from his sporran, and was liberally lubricating his vocal cords with the contents; Elvis was practising his stance and curled his top lip as if he had something stuck in his teeth; and Dolly was busy re-inflating her boobs with a bicycle pump.

Master of ceremonies, Jones the Butcher, dressed in his best suit for the occasion, looked more nervous than the contestants as he fingered the collar of what Crystal guessed was a new white shirt, still stiff and pristine. She thought his stringy neck sticking uncomfortably out of the collar gave him the appearance of an ill-at-ease turtle. "OK. Let's get this show on the road." He turned to the contestants with a strained smile, before stepping through the curtains to muted applause. "Welcome to Bala's Got Talent – the show where a star may be born," he announced with little conviction and a definite question mark in his voice. "As always, your applause on the clapometer decides the outcome." The clapometer in this case being Mavis, who served behind the cooked meat section of Mr Jones' shop.

"Anyway, let's get started with Huw – who has appeared in the show in all its guises over the years, and is our most senior contestant. Take it away, Huw – this could be your year."

The curtain opened just in time for the audience to spot Huw hiding away his flask. "Donald, where's yer trousers?" shouted one wag, but old stager Huw chose to ignore him as the backing track began to play.

He more or less ended in time with the music, and earned polite applause, but Crystal noticed as he stepped off stage that Huw's eyes seemed strangely glazed. She realised he was utterly pissed, and guided him to a chair in the wings, where he sat with legs splayed apart, oblivious to the world, and began to gently snore.

Next up was a juggler who dropped all his balls. Elvis split his trousers – and earned the biggest round of applause so far that night, and Dolly's boobs slowly deflated as she told the story of 'The Coat of Many Colors'. Crystal was feeling quietly confident when she and David were called to the stage.

They climbed onto a couple of tall stools, and as the music started, began to sing. Crystal gazed lovingly into David's eyes, and David stared back cross-eyed. She suppressed a giggle and managed to keep in time with the music. *David sounds pretty good*, she thought. *Hidden talents, that boy.*

The crowd fell silent, and as the music finished Crystal felt a second of panic. Then the applause started. Looking round, Crystal spotted many of the farming community who had turned up to support one of their own, clapping, cheering and stamping their feet. David turned and winked at her – crafty bugger.

"I think we've got it in the bag," whispered Crystal, standing with her back to the stage.

"I wouldn't be too sure," said David, gesturing over her shoulder.

A thin young girl in a wheelchair slowly propelled herself onto the stage, and reached out a frail hand to take the microphone from its stand. There was a collective "Aaaahhhh" from the audience, as the music started and the pale-faced waif began to sing the Titanic theme song, 'My Heart Will Go On'.

"That's us sunk," said David, as the child's wavering voice filled the hushed auditorium. "She doesn't have that great a voice but I doubt anyone cares."

Half the crowd began singing along, and Crystal saw that many of the women were openly weeping. Even some of the men wiped away a tear. The child ended her song with a weak smile and the audience rose as one in a standing ovation. Crystal could see that even if the clapometer was Mavis – who sold boiled ham and gala pies to her on a weekly basis – the chances of winning, for the rest of the contestants, had just been hit by an iceberg.

Crystal and David joined the applause as the child smiled, and weakly waved a spindly arm before she was wheeled off-stage by a large woman with peroxide blonde hair and tattoos on her sturdy arms, who had appeared from the wings. "Come on David," said Crystal. "Let's get out of these clothes. We're just in time to catch last orders in the pub. I'll buy you a consolation pint."

Crystal changed into her ordinary clothes, rather glad to put Cher into a Co-op carrier bag, and went to the Ladies to get the caked mascara from round her eyes.

As she entered, a young girl in a mini skirt and stiletto heels was applying carmine red lipstick at the mirror, and with a shock Crystal realised it was the girl in the wheelchair. "Congratulations on winning," she said. "What happened to the wheelchair?"

The teenager's made-up face contorted into something ugly. "Listen Grandma. It's about winning – and there's nowhere in the rules to say you can't use props. Just like that old tosser with a skirt and stick. It's a competition – get it? Duh," she said, pointing a finger to her head in a gesture that clearly meant she thought Crystal was an idiot. "Out the way, loser. I've got my winnings to collect." She brushed past Crystal and walked down the corridor, the click from her high heels echoing off the bare walls.

"It's not the winning, it's the taking part," shouted Crystal, to a retreating back.

"Yeah, right," came the reply.

Over a pint, Crystal related her encounter in the cinema lavvy to David and Old Huw, who had partly come round from his earlier alcohol-induced snooze and now nursed a pint of The Reverend James bitter. "Well, I suppose she had a point," said David. "I had some mates from the Farmers' Union over to give us a cheer, and I suppose you could say that was cheating a bit."

"God, David – you are always so reasonable. I suppose it's why I like you so much – that and the fact that it's your round. Same again for me, and I'll have a packet of crisps. Are you all right Huw? You've turned a bit green."

CHRISTMAS DAY

Crystal woke early – the alarm on the bedside table sounding unreasonably loud. She turned over to glance at the dial; 4am. "God, why did I ever talk myself into making Christmas dinner?" she moaned to herself as she reached for her dressing gown, pushed a tangle of hair back from her forehead and stepped into her new Builder's Bottom slippers – bought on a whim from the Christmas catalogue and a match for a pair of Marilyn Monroe Booby slippers bought for David.

She had prepared the turkey the night before, pushed butter under the skin and covered the bird in streaky bacon, with onions, garlic and a big bunch of sage placed inside the cavity, and carefully covered it in foil. Now all it needed was a long, slow cook.

Perkins shuffled on his perch, but remained silent, as Crystal turned on the oven and made herself a cup of tea whilst waiting for it to heat up. She looked at the huge bird sitting there in tin foil on the worktop. "I can't think why I got such a big bird for just four of us." It had looked so inviting sitting there all by itself in Mr Jones' shop that she couldn't resist it.

The smaller birds were already gone, and the 25-pounder was all he had left. "Sure it's a turkey, not a bloody ostrich?" Crystal joked. But Mr Jones wasn't known for his sense of humour, particularly where meat was concerned. "Lovely bird that, young Crystal. Brought it on myself in my own farm, free-range see, so it's grown big grubbing around in the hedgerows. Broad-breasted white is the variety – could have got to 50 pounds or more if I'd kept it to Easter, but it was already scaring the dogs. If you hadn't bought it, I'd have had it myself." He wistfully patted the bird's large breasts. "Have to make do with something else now."

Crystal manhandled the bird, along with a carrier bag full of sausage meat, chipolatas and streaky bacon, back to the car, and it had sat in her fridge until Christmas Eve.

Crystal finished her tea, and with some difficulty lifted the tray holding the bird into the oven, where it fitted snugly with barely an inch to spare. "Right, big boy. Back to bed for another couple of hours kip – then it's time to get the show on the road."

Crystal had invited David and his mother to have Christmas dinner at her lakeside cottage, and asked Huw as well when he fed her a sob-story about being all on his own over Christmas, as his son was going off with his mates to Benidorm. "OK Huw, but best behaviour. David's mother is coming, and I don't think she's very sure about me yet – whether to hate me or merely dislike me intensely. It's your job to keep her entertained."

When Crystal woke again she glanced at the alarm clock, and saw it was already past 8am. "Get moving girl. Lots to do before everyone arrives at midday."

Perkins was now wide-awake as Crystal headed downstairs, and the smell of cooking turkey was already filling the cottage with meaty aromas. "Happy Christmas, Perkins. I've got a lovely cuttlefish bone from the pet shop for you to nibble on."

"Can it, sweetheart." Perkins was still imitating the gangster movies Crystal had put on television to keep him amused while she worked.

Crystal carefully wrapped her presents, and put them under the tree – alarmingly expensive perfume for Mrs Owen, a bottle of Welsh malt whisky from the Penderyn distillery in Brecon for Huw, and a new shirt for David from the Armani shop in Manchester, along with a stocking full of very daft presents bought from the Santa's Sack catalogue, which he could open later when they were alone.

She spent the morning cooking. "Right. Prawn cocktail made and on the table, root veggy for the main course ready to go into the oven after the turkey comes out, Brussels sprouts ready to go. Christmas pud in the steamer. Cranberry sauce and pickles on the table. Perkins, I think we are ready. Party time."

Perkins replied with an uncanny rat-a-tat replication of a Thompson sub-machine gun.

* * *

Huw was first to arrive. A taxi pulled up to the front door and he emerged, dressed in his best weddings and funerals suit, and hobbled to the front door, waving his stick in farewell to the taxi as it reversed out onto the road.

"Hope I'm not too early? Got anything open yet?" he asked hopefully.

"Come in Huw. I'm sure I can find you something, but I'm sticking to tea myself. Don't want to be half-pissed when David's mum arrives. It wouldn't go down too well. Gin and tonic OK?"

"That would be very welcome, Crystal love." Huw settled into an armchair. "And how are you, Perkins boyo?"

"You talking to me? Who the f*** d'you think you're talking to?" answered Perkins.

Huw walked over to the perch where Perkins was sitting. "Still watching the Movie Channel I see."

"Sorry, you talking to me?" asked Crystal, walking in from the kitchen in her pinny. "What's funny? Did I say something funny?"

"No, just me and Perkins having a conversation. I see your other guests are arriving."

They looked out of the window, and saw David helping his mother out of his Ford pick-up.

Crystal opened the door. "Merry Christmas to you both. Come in and get warm by the log burner, Mrs Owen, it feels like it's freezing out there. You're in the car, David? Not going to be much fun for you if you can't have a drink."

David gave her a despairing look, and glanced at his mother, who had walked past Crystal without a greeting, and was settling into an armchair, a large black handbag clutched in both hands like a talisman to ward off evil.

Huw came to the rescue. "It's OK. I've got a taxi booked for four o'clock. I could drop you and your mum off if you like?"

David gave Huw a grateful look. "That would be great Huw. If you don't mind."

"Good, that's settled," said Crystal. "I'll open a bottle of bubbly. First of the day, eh?"

"Not for me," Mrs Owens declared. "I find it far too acidic. Don't suppose you have any Warninks advocaat? I don't mind a drop of that with lemonade."

Gordon Bennett, thought Crystal. *Pick the one thing I don't have, why don't you?* "No. But I do have some Baileys. Would that do?"

"I suppose so." Mrs Owen sniffed loudly as she looked round the room at Crystal's attempt at Christmas decorations with ill-disguised disdain.

"This is going to be a fun Christmas," muttered Crystal under her breath as she made drinks in the kitchen, and carried them out. She lofted her glass high in the air, and put on a forced smile. "Well, cheers everyone, and Happy Christmas."

"Cheers," replied David and Huw. Mrs Owens sipped her Baileys as if she had been given poison, and put it down on a side table.

"We'll eat in about half an hour if that's OK? In the meantime I thought we could open presents," suggested Crystal.

"That's not a real tree," announced Mrs Owen accusingly, as her hostile gaze turned to the tree in the corner, where all Crystal's presents were stacked.

"No, it's a bit of a tradition. I've had it for years and just keep it in a box in the attic and get it out every year," Crystal replied defensively.

"Surrounded by real trees so we are round here. If I'd known you were that hard up, I'd have got David to cut one for you and bring it down. He's here often enough."

"Well, anyway, here's your present Mrs Owen. And one for you, David and here you go Huw."

There was silence, apart from the crinkle of paper being unwrapped. "Just what I wanted," announced Huw. "Been dying to try this, thank you."

David was next: "Thanks love. Just what I needed for a special occasion."

Then Mrs Owen: "Very nice, thank you, but scent makes me come out in funny bumps, particularly the cheap stuff."

"Maybe you could just sort of sprinkle it on your clothes. Givenchy is a really good make, so you should be all right." Crystal suppressed the urge to scream. *Much more of this and she will be in bumps, David or no*, she thought.

Huw fished around in the carrier bag he had brought with him. "There you are Crystal. Happy Christmas." He passed over a heavy package.

"Thank you Huw." She tugged at the wrapping. "What can this be... oh... a can of paint... very... er, seasonal Huw. What's it for?"

"Noticed the other day that your front sash windows were looking a bit bare, where the weather's got to them. Need to keep an eye on that or the whole window frame could be rotten by the summer. Not like these plastic windows in new houses, see."

"Thanks, Huw. Very thoughtful. Is that present for me, David?"

"Yes, but I thought we might open our own presents later." David looked slightly embarrassed.

"Nonsense, let's have a look," said Crystal, grabbing the package and tearing one end open, seeing the Ann Summers packaging lurking inside. "On second thoughts, perhaps you're right. Later might be better." Couldn't see herself parading in her new trolleys in front of Huw and Mrs Owen, thank you very much. The image made her smile… and look forward to later that evening.

Mrs Owen reluctantly poked in her bag and handed Crystal a rather tatty package, wrapped in paper that looked like it had already been used more than once and sealed with masking tape. "Why thank you Mrs Owen. What can it be?"

Inside was a dull mustard coloured woollen scarf, which had seen better days and still had the £1.50 Oxfam price tag attached to it. "Thank you," said Crystal. "Just my colour, and you can't have too many scarves in winter round here. Perhaps you'd all like to go through to the dining room. The starter is already laid out. I'll be there in a minute after I look at how we're doing in the kitchen."

Crystal took the turkey out of the oven and stuck a meat thermometer in it to make sure it was cooked all the way through, replacing it with the root veg, stuffing and 'pigs in blanket' sausages. She left the turkey to stand in foil and re-joined her guests. "Everybody OK? What's wrong Mrs Owen?"

David's mother was looking at the prawn cocktail sitting in front of her like there was a live toad on her plate. "Sorry, I'm afraid I can't eat this. Prawns, you see. Make me heave. David, you can have mine." She shuddered and at arm's length pushed the plate towards David with her fingernails, as if merely touching the glass the offending prawns were sitting in would make her throw up.

"But you had a prawn curry from the takeaway last week, Mum," said David.

"Yes, but that was different. They were cooked and these are… pink. It's the texture, slimy like snails."

"Can I get you anything else?" Crystal asked – *a cup full of deadly nightshade, or eye of newt maybe?*

"No thank you. I'll just wait for the main course." Mrs Owen sat upright in her chair saying nothing, as the others ate in silence.

"Pass me the wine, David." Crystal poured herself a large glass of Muscadet, drinking half of it in one go. *Won't be able to do anything to please David's mum, so might as well just get pissed*, she decided.

Crystal went to check the oven – about another ten minutes and everything would be ready to go – and walked back to the dining room.

"Ran into Myfanwy the other day," Mrs Owen was saying as she came into the room. "Lovely girl. Went out with David for a while, if you remember?"

"We were eleven years old," said David. "It was hardly going out."

"Is that the Myfanwy from Llanuwchllyn?" asked Huw. "The big one? She could kick start tractors that girl. Got quite a mouth on her too, so I'm told. I heard she got into an argument with Big John in her local pub after he claimed he could shear a sheep faster than she could. Floored him with one punch so she did. I think you had a lucky escape there, David."

"I always liked her – one of the lads really, and we had some good times as I remember – just not the woman for me. Anyway, she's gay. Lives with a market gardener from Rhug," said David.

"You need a good sturdy lass on a farmyard. It's a hard life, and not right for everyone," Mrs Owen declared, looking directly at Crystal, who was busy finishing off the bottle of Muscadet.

Crystal decided she had taken just about enough from the old bat, and the wine was starting to have an effect on her inhibitions. "And I presume I don't measure up to that high standard, Mrs Owen?" Crystal asked, starting now on a bottle of Burgundy.

David and Huw suddenly got very interested in their plates, as the two women faced each other down. "Well, if I'm going to be perfectly honest, I don't think you are right for David. He needs someone a little younger. Someone who can give him children, and help on the farm – both of which you show no inclination of doing."

"Top of the world Ma. On top of the world," piped up Perkins from the front room.

"Thanks for your honesty – at least we know where we stand," said Crystal. "You're right. I'll never be a farm girl but *vive la différence* eh?" Crystal took another deep swig of her wine, and noticed the bottle at her end of the table was already nearly empty. "Excuse me, I'll get another bottle of red."

David had been quiet during the exchange, but now spoke up in a quiet but determined tone. "Let's call an end to this conversation right now please. I don't think it's very hospitable after Crystal's put herself out to invite us here today, to start on her in her own house.

"Sorry, Mum, but I'll choose who I go out with and as far as I'm concerned Crystal is the best thing that ever happened to me. Now let's just try and enjoy the rest of the day. Glass of wine, Huw?"

Both women sat with mouths open, and Huw took the opportunity to help himself to another large glass of Burgundy, his eyes darting from one to another of the little party, enjoying the drama – just like the Coliseum in Rome, he would later relate to his friends at the Glyndwr Arms.

Crystal served the main course, which was eaten in icy silence. Mrs Owen looked like she was about to say something on a couple of occasions, but remained silent, and Crystal had given up trying to be the hostess with the mostest. David and Huw just tucked in to the huge piles of food they had put on their plates. The Christmas pud came and went in a daze. She realised she had drunk far too much, but what the hell – it's only Christmas once. *Well, only once a year, so actually nearly forty Chrishmasses. God, even my thoughts are slurred*, she thought.

Mrs Owen left to go to the toilet, and Huw and David were making serious inroads into a bottle of Calvados – only twenty minutes left before the taxi was due, thank God. Crystal started unsteadily loading all the dishes into the dishwasher – couldn't stand the thought of having to do it later even if she was pissed. She looked over to where the turkey was sitting on the worktop, three-quarters of it still uneaten and wondered if the sheep in the field outside would eat it.

David came into the kitchen. "Need a hand with anything? Look, I just wanted to say sorry for Mum, she's not always like this but I'm an only child, and there's just the two of us now, so she can be a little protective. I don't think she understands our relationship, or what it means to me."

Crystal looked into his eyes – why could she see four of them?

"It's always a bit difficult for her at this time of year, since it was just before Christmas that Dad died, and she's virtually brought me up single-handed since then. She met Dad when she was only fourteen years old, and they were married on her sixteenth birthday. She's lived on the farm ever since, and she can't see a life beyond it, either for her or for me."

"I understand, but it doesn't make it any easier for me, David," Crystal finally managed to say, making an heroic effort to collect her thoughts. "Are you staying tonight by the way? I wish you would."

"I don't know. I can't really let her go home alone, but I'll walk back later when she's settled down for the night, if that's OK?"

"Of course it is, and I'll try to stay awake. Probably try to have a clear up. Give me a kiss you big old softie. When you get back we can have a dress rehearsal, if you know what I mean?"

They went back to the dining room, where Huw was sat by himself. His head drooped onto his chest and he was gently snoring – a half-full glass still in front of him.

"Can't think where your mum is. She went to the toilet ages ago. I'll go and see if she's OK." Crystal headed up the stairs. The toilet door was ajar, and she knocked gently. "Everything all right, Mrs Owen?"

She pushed open the door, and Mrs Owen was at the mirror, dabbing at her eyes with a tissue.

"Have you been crying? Listen, I'm sorry we had words, but whatever you think about me, and about my way of life – what I do for a living – you should know I'd never do anything to hurt David. I accept you and I may never be best of friends, and that you have reservations, but can we just agree to differ, and get on with things for David's sake?"

"You probably think me an awful old bat," Mrs Owen replied, tearfully. "I've not behaved well today, I know, and I've been sitting up here thinking on everything that's been said. Not taking anything back, mind, but David's made his choice and I'll have to learn to live with it. It's just not quite what I was wishing for him. You can see that can't you?" She extended a work-gnarled hand to Crystal, who took it gratefully, and the two women embraced – albeit briefly and awkwardly.

"Right, that's settled, you can help me downstairs Crystal. The stairs in this old cottage are a bit steep for me."

David looked worried when the two women walked down the stairs together. "Everything OK?"

"Why wouldn't it be?" said Mrs Owen sharply. "Get my coat, David. The taxi will be here in a minute. And you'd better wake Huw up. He looks like he's had a skinful."

As she was speaking Crystal saw headlights sweep into the drive. The taxi was right on time. David helped Mrs Owen into her coat, and Huw staggered to the door, his few remaining strands of hair sticking up from his head in an untidy grey halo. "Thanks Crystal. Lovely meal – best Christmas I've had for years. Noson dda."

As Huw headed unsteadily to the taxi, Mrs Owen turned to Crystal, and again extended her hand. "Thank you very much for inviting us," she said, with a glimmer of a smile.

Did she just wink at me? I'm sure she did, thought Crystal. *Either that or she has a facial tic.*

She embraced David and whispered, "I'll see you later. Don't be too long or I may be asleep, and we have presents to open – remember?"

"Trust me, it's all I'm thinking about," said David. "It could be a long night… "

THE BOXING MATCH

Crystal woke up shivering. The log burning stove in the front room had long since given up its warmth from the night before – and the bloody central heating system wasn't working properly again. Like her, it didn't seem to like getting started in the morning.

Wrapping the duvet round herself, Crystal wandered down to the kitchen and pushed the reset button on the ancient boiler – remembering as she did the words on the building survey she commissioned before buying the little cottage: "The boiler is at least twenty years old, and although it appears to be working satisfactorily at the moment, will probably need replacing at some point in the future."

The surveyor was just covering himself, she thought at the time. It was summer then, and didn't seem to matter very much. Her sister, Tish, had been trilling at her about what a beautiful setting it was on the shores of Lake Bala in North Wales, with the dramatic hills of Snowdonia as a backdrop blah… blah… but it was a warning that now sounded prophetic.

"Tish didn't tell me it was going to be friggin' freezing for more than half the year," she muttered to herself, as the boiler gave a reluctant 'woomph' and came to life – but for how much longer?

Perkins the parrot sat disconsolately in his cage. "It's OK, Perkins. Soon be toasty warm again."

"Cer I grafu," replied Perkins.

"Your Welsh is beginning to sound really good, Perkins. Not that I have any idea what you're saying half the time. Since Old Huw started his Welsh classes for us I can't seem to get my head around it, but you've taken to it like a duck to water – well a parrot anyway. Mind you, I think Huw's as bad as Jolyon for teaching you words I'd rather not know about."

Now she was up, Crystal decided to get to work on the stack of receipts and bills stuffed into a biscuit tin in a bottom drawer of her Welsh dresser – she'd put off sorting them out for months, but her accountant was now pressing for urgent action to avoid fines, and penalties up to and including the Tower of London and beheading, if they weren't on his desk by month's end. He told her in a rather bossy telephone call to give him time to be 'creative' before sending them off to Her Majesty's Revenue and Customs. *Bloody need to be as well*, thought Crystal, *or Perkins and I will be in the poor house.*

As Crystal sorted through her receipts, and totted up her proceeds on a pocket calculator, it became obvious that selling her paintings had been surprisingly lucrative. But where had all the money disappeared to? God, another huge tax bill loomed.

Disturbed from her labours by a knock at the door, she realised the duvet was still wrapped round her Beauty and the Beast jim jams – bought as a joke one Christmas, but so cosy and warm she now wore them throughout the winter – and her hair looked like overnight she'd turned into a manic red-haired Rastafarian.

Probably just the postie with a package – he's used to seeing me looking like a wreck, she reasoned. But on opening the door a stranger stood there: *Blimey, he's no postie*, she thought, shrinking into her duvet. Tall with long black hair, he had wide shoulders and slim hips, and was dressed all in black, with jeans, cowboy boots and, despite the weather, a tight T-shirt showing heavily muscled arms. A silver chain dangled in black curly chest hair. *He probably doesn't feel the cold or is really vain*, thought Crystal.

Almost certainly the latter since there was frost on the ground, but then he did seem to have quite a lot to be vain about. She imagined him regaling his friends with the story that he had met the mad Rastafari down by the lake. With a bit of luck he wanted a painting doing, and she could size him up properly to see if he was in proportion from top to bottom.

"Hello. Bore da," said the man, in a lilting Welsh accent. "Name's Madog – a lot of people call me Madog the Metal Man, on account of me being a blacksmith, and wrought iron artist. I've been hearing that your paintings have made quite an impact in Bala and, since we're both artists, I thought it was time I introduced myself. Believe you're walking out with my old pal, David. We went to school together you know, but I haven't seen him in a while. Anyway, how's the old bugger doing? Not so badly, looking at you."

Vain and a bullshitter, thought Crystal, mentally conjuring up the words 'hedge' and 'backwards' to adequately describe herself at the moment. "David's fine thanks, but what can I do for you, Madog? Sorry about the clothes, by the way – you caught me by surprise, and the boiler's been on the hop."

"Take a look if you want," said Madog, sidestepping past and inviting himself inside. "Bit of an all-rounder I am – got to be in these parts. If you stick the kettle on, I'll take a look see."

Fifteen minutes, two teas and half a packet of Hobnobs later, and Crystal had her answer: "Knackered if you ask me. Looks like the circuit board – which is going to cost you 250 quid minimum, and then there's fitting – even then you can't tell with these old boilers if that's going to sort it. Easier to get a new one. I could do a knock-down price of 700 quid or so."

Crystal's smile froze on her face, and her eyes opened wide – an image of herself looking like a dreadlocked Cherie Blair popped into her mind. She and Perkins would be frozen solid by spring.

"You look a bit taken aback, but I promise you it's a fair price. Have a think about it. Anyway, the main reason for the visit is to tell you about the Easter Craft Fair I help organise every year. To tell you the truth a lot of the stuff's a bit tatty – lots of home-knitted willy warmers, that sort of thing. I hoped you could come and give it a bit of class. It's well attended, so I think you'd be sure of a good bit of business out of it. I'll leave an information leaflet, and an application form. Phone number's on the bottom – just give me a ring if you want any more info, or just fancy a chat. I'm always available."

Bet you are, thought Crystal. *But this could be just what I need – a bit of cash for Easter.* "Yes thanks, Madog. I'd be very interested."

Crystal waved Madog off, as he drove from the lane outside in a new-looking red Mercedes GL. *Must be doing all right for himself*, thought Crystal, looking at her slightly scuffed old Honda Jazz sitting in the driveway at the front of the cottage. Hearing a baaaaing noise she walked to the side of the house, to where her pet, Skippy, waited by the fence – now the only sheep in the field until a new flock arrived with their mothers.

"How are we doing, Skippy?" The sheep ran towards her bleating as if he had been abandoned for a month.

Skippy should have been lamb chops by now, but Crystal had adopted him during the summer, when the field was full of sheep owned by local farmer, Ted. "I'll feed you in a minute. Just let me get some clothes on," said Crystal, smiling as she remembered how she came to own Skippy. He was one of a flock of lambs that frequently wandered onto the rail track at the bottom of the field. There was a fence but they always seemed to find a way through – usually led by Skippy. Crystal's daily task during the summer had been to rescue them and get them back into the field, but Skippy had other ideas – surprising both of them by performing a spectacular jump over Crystal's shoulder to avoid capture. Eventually he was tempted back into the field but only by bribing him with food.

Since then he was always at the fence to greet her when she came into her garden, and the two had struck up a relationship.

Impulsively, when the lambs were about to be herded into a cattle truck for slaughter, Crystal had offered to buy Skippy and handed Ted £75 in cash – the proceeds of selling a pen-and-ink sketch of the lake to a tourist the day before. Now a nearly grown hoggit, she wondered if it was kind to keep Skippy by himself – but better lonely than dead, and she couldn't afford to keep two sheep. Guiltily, she wondered if Skippy may have to be sacrificed to help pay the bills – but dismissed the thought. She'd manage somehow.

Soon he'd get his first shearing. Crystal looked forward to giving the wool to big sis, Tish, to weave, and turn into a Nordic-noir sweater, so she could walk the streets of Bala in the autumn looking suitably gloomy and pouty. "It's a better look than duvet chic, eh Skippy? My hair looks a bit like yours at the moment."

Crystal looked at her watch. "Blimey. Look at the time. I'd better get dressed before it's lunchtime already. I'm not likely to impress would-be clients less they be fellow Rastafari," said Crystal in a faux-Jamaican accent as she walked into the house.

* * *

David turned up that evening, flopped down on the sofa with a groan and kicked off his shoes. "What a day. Been out mending fences – up to my knees in mud and cow shit. Put the kettle on 'ey love."

Good of you to ask. I've had a lovely day personally, thought Crystal, but said, "Met a friend of yours today – Madog the Metal Man. He sends his regards."

"What did he want?" David said sharply, surprising Crystal with his offish tone.

"Just asking me to take part in the Easter Craft Fair. Why, what's wrong? He said he was a friend of yours."

"Nothing wrong. We went to school together, that's all. We're certainly not friends – wouldn't touch him with a barge pole personally, and I'd advise you to treat him the same."

"Why? What's wrong with him?"

"Just something that happened a long time ago – not worth talking about now. Let's just say he's not very trustworthy. So what sort of a day have you had?"

And that was that – there was something David wasn't telling her about the relationship between him and Madog. Stubborn bugger when he wanted to be – but she'd get it out of him sooner or later.

David, however, refused to be drawn about Madog, and as the weeks went by the subject was forgotten – until a chance encounter at the Glyndwr Arms.

Crystal took the head off a pint of ice-cold lager, wiping her mouth with the back of her hand with satisfaction. "Just finished another landscape of the lake – my best yet. I'll have quite a collection to exhibit at the Easter Fair – along with the usual batch of nudes of course. Can't forget the buttocks and bollocks – it's still what brings in most of the—"

She saw David glaring across the room with a fixed stare. "Just what I need – fuckin' Metal Mickey!"

Crystal followed his gaze to where Madog was standing by the bar, dressed in his trademark all-black attire. "You don't usually swear, David. What's wrong?"

Madog turned and waved, walking over with his pint. "Hello, David. Crystal. Hardly recognised you with your clothes on." Crystal blushed slightly, and ignored David's inquiring look. "How's it going? Mind if I join you?" Madog ignored the frosty response from David, and pulled up a chair anyway. "See you signed up for the Easter Fair, Crystal. Still chasing sheep round the hills at the back of that farm of yours, David?"

Before he could respond to the obvious put-down, Madog turned to Crystal. "We go back a way, David and me. Misspent youth chasing girls when we weren't chasing a ball round the rugby field, eh David? He was always getting into trouble, getting beat-up on a Saturday night. I had to come and rescue him, remember that?"

"I remember it was you that usually started the trouble, then left before it kicked off," said David.

"Not quite how I recall it," replied Madog evenly. "We were in the local boxing club too, but David never got the hang of making his fists and legs move at the same time – there was that time I downed you in the first round?"

David bridled. "Lucky punch. Wouldn't happen again."

"Now boys," said Crystal. "Let's all play nicely. What have you been up to recently, Madog?"

He ignored her and continued to stare at David. "Fancy your chances, David? The boxing club's still open, and we could have a return match. You'll need to lose a bit round the old waist first though – getting a bit tubby to be truthful – and I wouldn't want to take advantage. That old mum of yours must be feeding you too well."

Crystal looked at David, and saw his jaw set in the stubborn way she had noticed before, that meant no matter what she said he was determined to go his own way. "Just name the day and time, and I'll be there. Now, I have a busy day tomorrow – chasing sheep as you say. You coming Crystal?"

She hardly had time to finish her pint, which she quickly gulped down as David headed for the door. Madog had a smug look on his face, and winked leerily at her as she hurried after David.

Crystal struggled to keep pace with David as he strode ahead across the causeway. "What the bloody hell are you playing at? Talk to me. What is it that gets you about Madog? And why did you let yourself get talked into a fight? He looks pretty big to me and I'm worried you're going to get hurt."

"Don't worry. I can look after myself," said David defensively, but slowed his pace and took her hand. "It goes back a long way. It's true that we used to be friends, but he was always bloody arrogant and self-centred. Never gave a thought for anyone else. A pal of mine, Charlie, was going steady with a girl called Alice. Madog decided he liked her too, and didn't give up till he had her. Broke Charlie's heart, and a few months later he joined the army – didn't see any future in Bala any more, you see. A year on and he was dead – blown up by a landmine in Iraq. Madog had already dumped Alice and moved on by that time. I don't suppose it was directly his fault, but I never forgave him – he knows it too. Just likes to take the piss, pretending we're still good friends, when he knows I can't stand the sight of him.

"He's already come knocking at your door, and trust me it's only a matter of time before he makes a move on you. Well this time I'm going to get in first, and give him the hiding I should have given him years ago."

Crystal didn't say anything – what would have been the point? She could see he was determined. But she remembered the first-round knockout, and hoped history wasn't about to repeat itself.

* * *

The day of the fight drew near. Crystal hadn't seen David for nearly a week – except when she saw him jogging past the cottage with a fixed expression – not even as much as a wave. *Probably playing 'Eye of the Tiger' in his head. Heading to the Mound, to run up and give a jubilant cheer when he gets to the top,* she thought. He wasn't looking much like Rocky Balboa though – more like Forrest Gump in shorts. "In training. See you after the fight on Saturday," was the terse message left on her answerphone after she called to see how he was getting on, and to see if he fancied coming round that evening.

Anyway, Crystal still had work to do. Her accounts had finally been scanned and sent for creative vetting by the accountant in Manchester, and Crystal could now devote her time to building her collection of pictures. The new landscapes were mainly acrylic paintings of the lake, Llyn Tegid, in many of its moods, from winter with snow-covered mountains as a backdrop, to spring when the snow had receded to the very tops of the peaks, and lambs had begun to appear in the green fields below. Today a chill breeze was blowing along the lake, ruffling its waters, and low clouds obscured some of the higher peaks.

She was interrupted halfway through her latest canvas by Old Huw knocking on the front door. Outside his son sat in a battered old pick-up, and as Crystal opened the door the smell of the stable yard invaded her nostrils. "What the bloody hell have you got there, Huw? It doesn't 'alf pen an' ink."

Huw swatted at a swarm of flies with his cap. "Manure. Best in the county. Just what you need for that rhubarb patch you're starting. Young Gandalf here's been working at the stables, and when I heard they had half a ton of muck going spare, I thought of you. Where do you want it?"

"Don't tempt me, Huw. Just stick it round the back, as far from the house as you can get it."

Gandalf expertly manoeuvred his pick-up round the side of the house, ignoring Huw's arm-waving and attempts to direct him, and stepped out from the driver's cab, picking up a large shovel from the footwell. "Thanks, Gandalf. You Welsh men bring me the nicest presents. I'll see you and the hobbit inside for a cup of tea when you're finished," said Crystal, pausing as she had a thought: "Tell me. I hope I'm not being rude but is Gandalf really your name? It doesn't sound particularly Welsh."

"No. Used to have long hair and a beard back in the day, and Huw started calling me Gandalf – old bugger thought it was funny. The name stuck, and now that's what most people call me – it's really Gwyndaf, by the way."

Ten minutes later and both men appeared at the kitchen door. "Boots off, please," said Crystal, looking at their manure-caked footwear. When she saw that the rest of their clothes weren't in a much better state she sat them on the wipe-down wooden chairs.

"Pen an' ink, pen an' ink," piped up Perkins from the lounge.

"Have some tea, and Welsh cakes," said Crystal, laying out her home-made fare on the dining room table. "Made them yesterday, and though I say so myself, they've turned out pretty well."

"Pice ar y maen. That's what Welsh cakes are called round here," said Huw between bites. "So that's your Welsh lesson for the day out of the way. You hear that Perkins? You'll be at the boxing match on Saturday, I presume, Crystal – to support David when he gives the Metal Man a good hammering?"

"I don't like boxing. Bit brutal for me. But of course, I'll be there to support him – even if I think he's bloody stupid to get into the ring with someone the size of Madog."

Huw helped himself to another Welsh cake. "Not bad for a first attempt. A few more sultanas and they'd be near perfect," he judged, wiping a crumb from his upper lip. "Anyway, David will be fine. Matter of fact Gandalf and me are going to be his corner men. I was quite a handy flyweight in my youth you know. Represented North Wales in the all-Wales finals in 1956, and Gandalf could handle himself in the ring before he became a pot-smoking long-haired hippy."

Gandalf lifted his eyes to the ceiling, but said nothing.

"What happened at the finals? Did you win?" asked Crystal.

"No. Took a total pasting from a Swansea lad," admitted Huw ruefully. "I was only sixteen at the time, and he was nearly four years older than me mind.

"Trust me. David's in good hands. What could go wrong when you have a team like this?" beamed Huw, waving his hands expansively round the room.

"Granted, Madog's a cage fighter with a bit of a reputation. The Beast of Bala they call him when he fights – but David's got guts and determination, and he's been training for weeks now. I've been with him down at the leisure centre nearly every day, and shown him a few old tricks from my youth. How to run mostly… don't worry, I'm only joking." He patted Crystal's knee.

"Cage fighter? No one told me that. Oh my God, he's going to get slaughtered." Crystal cradled her head in her hands. "David, what have you done?"

* * *

Fight night arrived. It was a warm Friday evening, so Crystal and Tish decided to walk into town for the big grudge match that had become the talk of the area. Although both knew Bala pretty well by now, they had to ask directions to the boxing club, which turned out to be in a single-storey building with a corrugated roof, tucked at the back of the council estate – more like a big shed really. Both had ringside seats for the fight – fold-down wooden chairs that looked like they had seen better days, and which Crystal found creaked alarmingly every time she moved. The small building was rapidly filling up, and she saw Madog had brought a large fan club of burly tattooed men with him, many clutching cans of beer and chanting "Metal Man, Metal Man – Who Can Win, Only He Can Can," followed by loud cheers. She and Tish were the only women there, and the atmosphere felt threatening. The smell of liniment, stale sweat, mildew and testosterone hung heavy in the air, like an approaching thunderstorm. "If this kicks off, duck and head for the door – I'll be right behind you," Tish whispered. "Look, there's David."

Crystal turned and saw David, with Huw and Gandalf falling into step behind him, emerge from a door marked 'Toilets and Changing Rooms'. The sight of him gave Crystal hope – he looked pretty good in his red shorts and boxing gloves, and had lost a bit of weight from round the middle. Not exactly ripped, but not bad. Tish was standing, waving an arm and chanting "Ooooo Oooooo Oooooo," but the rest of the crowd remained silent. Crystal smiled weakly, and felt a little faint. David looked in her direction, nodded, and ducked under the ropes into the ring, while Gandalf helped Old Huw up the steps to the corner.

Then Madog stepped out, and the crowd roared. It was obvious who the favourite was. Dressed in sequined black shorts, Crystal saw with dismay that he looked like a white version of Mike Tyson – bigger if anything – toned and muscular. He danced toward the ring, high-fiving his friends, and punching the air as if the fight had already been won. Spotting Crystal, he waved, and blew a kiss in her direction, which she chose to ignore.

Gripping one of the corner posts Madog jumped, with surprising agility for a man of his size, over the top rope into the ring, glancing over to David with a smug 'can you do that?' look on his face.

The referee called the two men to the middle of the ring, Madog a head taller than David as they stood toe-to-toe, staring impassively at each other as the ref gave the usual lecture – no biting, holding, head-butting or gouging, shake hands etc etc… They touched gloves and returned to their respective corners, the bell rang and the fight was on.

Madog rushed out fists flying – three-quarters of the way across the ring before David had moved. "Cover, cover," shouted Huw from the corner, as David raised his arms to block the blows raining in from Madog – he was already on the ropes.

"Break," shouted the referee and Madog reluctantly backed off. David stepped forward, launching a tentative punch at Madog's head, which was easily deflected. But David kept on coming. Crystal saw that Madog had been right – David moved, punched, moved, but never both at the same time.

Madog, for his part, settled down and seemed content to keep his distance, dance around, and launch punches at the smaller man using his longer reach to full advantage. Some of the blows had clearly found their mark. The bell sounded and both men went to their corners. Crystal noticed David was already bruised round the eyes and had red marks around his rib cage. As he slumped onto his stool, Huw whispered urgently into his ear. Madog remained standing, chatting over the ropes to his pals by the ringside.

The bell went and it was round two. Madog danced out, giving the crowd his Ali-shuffle, while David stood fists up, watching, as Madog danced closer, still playing to the crowd. The punch came from nowhere, snapping Madog's head back. David stepped forward now, step – punch – step, as Madog backpedalled, shaking his head to clear it. Crystal was on her feet. "Yes…go on… fuckin' hammer him… oh… er … sorry… got carried away. Good punch that. Jolly good." Tish was pulling at her kaftan. "Sit down sis… remember we're a bit outnumbered."

Madog was saved by the bell, and when the third round started he appeared less confident, more careful. David's lumbering style seemed to be paying off, as he stalked Madog round the ring. Both men were landing punches, but Madog had lost all his swagger. David was looking more confident and Madog was by now on the defensive.

By the fourth round David had Madog backed into the ropes, and was pounding him with lefts and rights. The referee called "break" and ordered David back to his corner while he stepped forward to examine a cut over Madog's left eye.

David obeyed the referee's instruction and turned to go back to his corner. Without warning Madog pushed the ref aside and launched himself at David, who turned, but too late, and was caught by a devastating right hook to the jaw. Crystal gasped in horror as David was lifted from the canvas by the blow, before collapsing in a heap. His gumshield flew off and landed with a blood-and-spit splat in her lap. There was a second's stunned silence in the room, as everyone took in what had happened – then the boos started. The crowd turned against their local hero and even Madog's fan club joined in, or stood shaking their heads in disbelief. Madog ducked under the ropes and headed back to the changing rooms, shouting at the baying crowd, "Winner – I'm the winner. It was his fault he was looking away. Nothing in the rules to say I did anything wrong." But no one was listening, and boos still echoed round the hall long after Madog was out of sight.

Huw knelt next to David, and wafted smelling salts under his nose, as Crystal climbed into the ring. David coughed, and opened his eyes, finally focusing on Crystal's face. "What happened? Did I win?"

Crystal brushed away a tear. "In my eyes, yes you did, you bloody idiot. Just promise me you won't get into a boxing ring again."

* * *

The Monday after the fight, and Crystal was working in her studio, creating from memory a painting of the epic clash – particularly Madog's underhand blow. It was a present for David, to remind him of his promise not to be so bloody stupid in the future. She particularly liked the slow motion spray of spit and blood propelling the gumshield from his mouth, and the look of horror and disgust on her own face as it landed in her lap. It was a warm day and the door was open, as she saw a familiar-looking red Mercedes pull up outside the cottage.

Madog got out, still showing the bruises from the fight, and walked round the side of the house to the open studio door. "You've got a cheek showing up here. What do you want?"

Madog gave her a lop-sided grin – what she presumed he thought was his little boy lost look. "Well, I did win the fight, and I thought to the winner the spoils, so to speak, so here I am to collect my prize."

"You'll not be collecting anything here, Madog," said Crystal. "What you did was not only unsporting, but cowardly. David could have been seriously hurt. I don't know what you were fighting about, but it certainly wasn't about me. I'm not some sort of prize to be handed out, so I'll ask you to leave."

"And what if I don't?" said Madog, his face contorting into an ugly leer. "Of course you were what the fight was about. What else?"

He grabbed her arm in a vice-like grip and started to propel her backwards into the studio, as Crystal writhed, trying to break free. "Get your hands off me," she shouted, aware that the cottage was remote from neighbours and any chance of help.

Apart from the two of them struggling on the step there was only Skippy in the field, who looked up from his grazing when he heard raised voices.

Over Madog's shoulder, Crystal heard Skippy give a deep "baaaa" that she had never heard before – more like a guttural growl. He began to run towards the wire fence separating the field from Crystal's little plot of land, picked up speed, and cleared it in one magnificent leap.

Madog was too intent on what he was doing to realise what was happening behind him. Crystal managed to twist free just as Skippy – now running at full tilt – caught him in the middle of the back. Madog squealed in surprise – a rather girly sound it struck Crystal – as Skippy's horns connected propelling him forward a full 10 feet, to land face-first in Huw and Gandalf's manure heap, with a wet splat. "Right place for you," said Crystal, looking down at Madog, who attempted to get up, but fell again into the slippery pile. Horseflies buzzed round his head, which was crowned by a particularly big dollop of horse turd, which slid slowly down the side of his face. "Looks like the shit's in the shit. I'm ringing David now, so if I were you I'd make myself scarce, because if he arrives and you are still here I wouldn't like to be responsible for what he does," said Crystal, reaching for her mobile and stepping inside the cottage in case Madog still had some fight left in him. "As my friend Skippy here would say if he could only talk, 'butt out buddy'".

FRIENDS COME TO VISIT

THE TOURIST
ISSUE 346

In this issue we focus on the pretty Welsh market town of Bala, set amid spectacular scenery in the Snowdonia National Park – and rapidly becoming a number one attraction for activity holidays.

This beautiful part of Britain is home to sailing, walking, climbing, white-water rafting, mountain biking, zip wires and zorbing, all on the doorstep of this historic little town of less than 3,000 people, lying at the north end of Bala Lake.

The lake is known to Welsh-speaking locals – about 80 per cent of the population – as Llyn Tegid, and is the largest natural lake in Wales, popular with sailors and watersport enthusiasts alike.

It lies in the shadows of two major mountain ranges with summits nearly 3,000ft high, making it a popular hotspot for serious walkers and climbers virtually all year round. To the south of Bala is the Aran mountain range with fourteen summits, and to the north-east the Berwyn range with twenty-four peaks and Wales' highest waterfall.

A series of footpaths make it possible to walk round the lake. It's a fourteen-mile slog, but the distance can be cut by almost five miles by taking the narrow gauge Lake Railway part of the way, from Llanuwchllyn to Bala.

And there is no shortage of places to stay, with two campsites, a hotel and numerous bed and breakfast and backpacker hostels. There are also many self-catering holiday lets near to the town centre, and becoming very popular in the area is Airbnb, where local people invite you into their homes as paying guests...

* * *

Crystal put down her newsletter, and turned in the bed to David. "Story here from the tourist association mag mentions Airbnb. Quite interesting. I could give it a try – make a few extra quid, which would come in useful to pay the taxman."

There was no reply from the other side of the bed, apart from a non-committal grunt. "What are you reading? Anything good?"

David put down the magazine he was reading. "North West Hill Farmer Today. It's an interesting article about ticks – quite a problem in Wales, seeing as there are so many sheep, and they can spread some nasty diseases. Mad Ted got one in, shall we say, a very sensitive place last summer. No idea how it got there – better not ask in some cases, particularly with Ted – but he had to have it surgically removed and he was on antibiotics for a month. We call him 'Tick Tock' now on account of where it was on his— "

"Yes, thanks David. Too much information sometimes. Anyway, just to warn you, I spoke to Freddie earlier, and she and Nigel are visiting this weekend – it's ages since I've seen them. I know you don't like them very much, but they are my best friends, and I think if you got to know them, you'd realise they are really nice people, if a little brash.

"You've suddenly gone awfully quiet, and a bit stiff – but not in a nice way," said Crystal, reaching under the bedclothes, with a wicked grin on her face. "See what we can do about that, eh?"

David tried to resist but responded despite himself to Crystal's touch. "Just find them a bit, you know, loud. Ow! Fingernails."

"If I make it worth your while, will you at least try?" asked Crystal, as she rolled on top of David.

There was a muffled response: "Give it a go, I suppose."

* * *

The weekend dawned, and David had reluctantly agreed to be there to meet and greet. He sighed at the sound of the couple's old Mercedes rumbling into the driveway outside Crystal's cottage. "Get that bloody wine open and be quick about it by 'eck," he exclaimed loudly, in a poor imitation of Nigel's flat Mancunian vowels.

"Behave," said Crystal. "Remember, if you want Mr Willy to have a happy time tonight, you'll be nice and make the effort."

Seconds later and the door flew open as Freddie exploded into the room. "Darling, it's been ages. Kiss, kiss. Come and snog me David – no tongues like last time."

Crystal sensed David wince, but he gamely stepped forward into Freddie's embrace. "How are you Freddie?" he asked, with some difficulty as his face was being smothered with wide-lipped full-on kisses.

Freddie let out a jackal-like laugh that rebounded off the walls of the little cottage. "Oooh, I could just eat you up, David." Next door, in the lounge, Perkins repeated the laugh with uncanny clarity.

Seconds later Nigel staggered through the door clutching what seemed to be half the contents of their Manchester home in an array of bags, cases and suit holders. "Rest's in the car, including the wine. Got any open, by the way? It looks to me like t'sun's just over the yardarm."

David and Crystal both suppressed a smile. "It's only three o'clock," said Crystal. "I thought we could have a cup of tea and a cake, and wander over into Bala for early doors about five. I've a table booked at Plas-Yn-Dre at seven, if that's OK with everyone? Tish and her husband, George, are meeting us there."

Nigel momentarily looked grumpy. "Suppose so. I'll get the rest of the stuff from the car, and lock it up – can't be too careful, even in Bala."

"Not sure who'd want to steal a bloody old banger like that," said Freddie, helping herself to a large slice of bara brith and munching noisily. "Don't know why we can't get a new car, he can afford it for God's sake, but he insists the old Merc's a classic. Tight old bastard."

David cast a glance out of the window. One of the very few things he liked about Nigel was the car, which he had to admit looked impressive on the driveway, its silver metallic paint and chrome gleaming in the sunshine. Big V8 engine to boot, which made it sound like a low flying aircraft coming over the bridge.

Crystal followed David's gaze. "Boys and their toys, eh David? Why don't you give Nigel a hand, while Freddie and me start to get ready?"

David reluctantly obeyed – meeting Nigel as he struggled towards the door with a case of wine. Two more cases stood by the open car boot. "Never 'ave enough wine. That's what I say, and you can't exactly nip round t'corner to the offie here."

Crystal followed them onto the drive and saw a farm wagon had pulled up at the gate to the field next door. Lambs and their mothers were being disgorged by 'Tick Tock' Ted. Skippy had run to his side of the wire fence to greet the new arrivals, who milled around making loud baaaing noises as they accustomed themselves to their new surroundings.

Behind her there was a screech which reached a similar decibel level to a jumbo jet on take-off, or one of the RAF fighter planes that made frequent low-level passes over the lake. "Aren't they cute?" the last word elongated to sound like the Arabian state of Kuwait. "Look at the little babies," exclaimed Freddie, in a little-girl voice at odds with a 6-foot tall, forty-something woman in full make-up and stilettos, on which she teetered unsteadily as she tottered to the fence. "Can I stroke one? Please," she implored Ted, who stared at her as if she were some sort of alien creature.

"All be piled up on Mr Jones' counter come August," David offered, but shut up when Crystal glared pointedly at him, and then at his nether regions.

"Hello Ted. Another flock of lambs for me to look after for the summer then?"

Ted stood bandy-legged on the ramp to the cattle truck, giving a wayward sheep who didn't want to get out a hefty thwack round the rump with a stick he was carrying. "If you don't mind, Crystal, it'd be most welcome. I'll leave you some feed to tempt them back in if they get onto the railway track again. Just ring me if there are any problems. See yon Skippy's getting big. Make a fine ram that one. Bit sorry I sold him to you now, but I might be asking you to lend him to me for a bit of tupping."

Given Tick Tock's reputation, an image jumped into Crystal's mind she found hard to dispel. "I'm sure he'd be delighted, Ted, as long as they've been properly introduced to each other before courting starts."

The joke fell flat with Ted. "Won't need no introduction. Just point him in the right direction, and he'll be up and at 'em. Ain't no messing once a ram gets the smell. Look at old Bessie there." Ted pointed to a sheep that was wandering round in circles being followed by three lambs, and which Crystal noticed only had one eye.

"Best breeder we have, despite her age. Sometimes has two sets of lambs in a year that one, on account she can't see them coming at her from the blind side. Up and in before she knows what's hit her. No chance to run off then. Not that daft rams, I reckons."

Freddie by this time had discarded her shoes, and was running round the field in a futile attempt to capture a lamb. "Is yon mad lady with you?" asked Ted. "She's starting to frighten my sheep."

"It's OK, Ted. We're going in now. FREDDIE… come on now… they shoot sheep worriers round here you know."

* * *

The noise level at Plas-Yn-Dre hit new highs as bottles of wine were passed to and fro. Tish's husband, George, noisily addressed the problem of property investment in city hotspots with Nigel, and Crystal, Tish and Freddie recalled tales of old pals and nights out in Manchester – Freddie's fog horn laugh turning heads at the other tables. The waitress, with a smile frozen onto her face, waited politely for their orders, and David buried his head in the menu, taking great interest in the small print about the restaurant's opening hours.

More wine, and main courses, were at last chosen, and the noise level dropped to merely loud as the food began to arrive. "Best steaks in Wales here," announced George to no one in particular.

David perked up – at last a subject he knew something about. "Good local meat – straight from an ancient breed of Welsh black cattle, hung for a minimum of— " he was cut short by Freddie, who put her hands on her head with two fingers in the air, to imitate horns, and made a loud 'mooo' noise, followed by the signature cackle – cut short as her hand flew to her mouth. "Whoops. Think I've just had a little accident. Excuse me – just have to go to the little girl's room to tidy myself up."

She headed unsteadily towards the door marked 'Toilets', followed by Crystal. "Back in a minute. I'll just make sure she's OK. If the meal arrives before we get back, can someone ask for some mustard – Dijon if they've got it, or English. Not that sweet German stuff."

Nigel turned to David. "Sorry about that. Probably pissed herself – happens sometimes when she gets a bit over excited. I know we're a bit loud – particularly Freddie – and a bit manic. Daft thing is I can hear myself and Fred, and I know we're going a bit over the top. City living I suppose – have to shout to be heard over the crowd. Anyway, we'll be out of your hair after tomorrow, and you and Crystal can get on with life. You've been good for her y'know – the last one was a total twat, and for ages everyone could see it apart from her. Luckily, she finally came to her senses and got rid."

David felt a bit guilty for his earlier thoughts about Nigel, but he was unsure how to answer. Maybe he wasn't such a bad bloke after all. "Thanks. Crystal and I are very different. She's much more outgoing and impulsive than me, but it seems to work for us."

Crystal and Freddie returned to the table, and soon the noise levels were back to heavy metal levels, as brandies were drunk, money for the bill counted out, and farewells made to the relieved diners at other tables – one of whom had a lipstick kiss planted on his bald head by Freddie as she left.

Outside on the street, they waved off George and Tish, who had pre-booked a taxi to take them back up the hill to their farmhouse, and set off walking back to Crystal's house, Freddie still teetering on her high heels and proclaiming loudly how bloody quiet it was in the countryside. Suddenly, she veered to one side and fell over a low stone wall, into the garden of a house, where she flailed helplessly in a flower bed. Nigel stepped over the wall, and with a surprising show of strength born from long practice, picked her up in a fireman's lift. "Sorry, she goes quite suddenly. Fine one minute and hopelessly bladdered the next."

He continued walking towards the causeway, with a now lifeless Freddie hanging limply over his shoulder. "Might have to give me a hand after a bit, David. Or we could just drag her between us – she wouldn't know anything about it. Doesn't feel a thing when she's like this. Virtually comatose, but at least we can all get a bloody word in edgeways."

Silence descended in the cottage, as Freddie was dumped unceremoniously upstairs, and everyone made their way to bed, David last as he carefully brushed his teeth and flushed the loo – keenly expectant of his promised well-earned reward for putting up with the visitors. On entering the bedroom he saw Crystal face down, and snoring loudly. A low fart rumbled from beneath her Beauty and the Beast jim jams. "Who said romance was dead?" he muttered, as he got in beside her and turned out the light.

* * *

Breakfast the next morning was a subdued affair. David had left early to tend to his animals. Even Freddie had run out of anything to say. Nigel, however, seemed positively cheerful, and had already donned full walking gear. "Thought we'd wander up t'hill that's a few feet short of a mountain to see your friend Sylvie, or catch that tooty train to the next village, and walk up t'hill there." He helped himself to another piece of black pudding from the plate in the middle of the table. "You eating that, Freddie?" He looked at her plate of uneaten eggs and bacon.

"Sorry, back in a minute," said Freddie, lurching suddenly upstairs and slamming the toilet door behind herself.

"Waste not, want not," announced Nigel, heaping her food onto his already full plate. "What's that sheep doing?" He pointed out of the window to the field behind the cottage.

"Oh no," said Crystal. "She's caught in some barbed wire. I'll have to ring David, or Ted if he's around."

"Not to worry. Super-Nigel is here and ready to go to the rescue."

He bounded out of the cottage followed by Crystal, who could see it was one-eyed Bessie that was caught in the wire, her lambs bleating loudly by her side.

"Be careful Nigel," warned Crystal, but he scaled the wire fence and strode across the field towards the pitifully bleating sheep, intent on performing his good deed of the day.

"Soon have you out of there old girl," he said. Bessie looked less than impressed and kept struggling, as Nigel grabbed hold of her fleece and tugged at the wire. Bessie struggled and twisted in tight circles, as Nigel clung on like a rodeo-rider. She finally pulled free from the wire, and wandered off with her lambs as if nothing had happened. Nigel, however, was now hopelessly entangled. "Sorry. I think I'm in a bit of a pickle, Crystal."

Crystal fished out her mobile phone. "Hi, David. You know you were out mending fences the other day. Do you still have the wire clippers you were using handy?"

Half an hour later, and a bloodied and bruised Nigel was free – and standing naked in the bath while David and Crystal dabbed at his wounds with cotton wool soaked in antiseptic. "Sorry about this," said Nigel. "Don't think I'm quite cut out for life in the countryside."

"Still," he said, instantly cheering up. "Great tale to tell the blokes in the office on Monday morning – along with a few embellishments of course. How I saved a flock of sheep from flinging themselves off a cliff at great personal risk to myself – that sort of thing."

"Shut up, Nigel," said Crystal, who continued dabbing. "I'll leave those bits round the front end to you if you don't mind, David?"

As Nigel turned to accept David's tender ministrations, Crystal clapped her hands to her face and laughed. "I'm sorry, I know it's not really funny but is that what I think it is?" she said, pointing to Nigel's left buttock, where a large brown tick had attached itself.

Nigel craned his neck, to try and look at what the object of interest was. "Someone mind letting me in on the joke? What are you both laughing about?"

David managed to suppress his laughter. "Seems Nigel is now Tick Tock Two – well nearly since it's not in quite the right place. Tick Bot One, I suppose! Outpatients in Wrexham for you I'm afraid, my friend. You have a gift from Wales that I think you will want to get rid of."

Nigel was bent double, holding a shaving mirror between his legs, with Crystal and David giggling in the corner, when Freddie walked into to the bathroom. "What's all the laughing about? You guys nearly finished? I'm dying for a pee. What are you doing Nigel? And what's that little mushroomy thing on your arse?"

Pulling himself to his full height, Nigel announced grandly: "Actually, my dear, it's a badge of honour – a memento of my heroic sheep rescue, which – when it is removed – I'm going to have framed and put on our kitchen wall. In the meantime, I believe we're going to have to take a small detour to Wrexham on the way home."

BARE IN BALA

Crystal gazed across the wide expanse of water, her artist's eyes noting the lake's ever-changing mood – dark one minute, then light with reflections as billowing white clouds drifted across the powder-blue sky. Changing again as a light breeze ruffled the surface.

It had been nearly eight months since she moved into the lakeside cottage. It was mid-summer then, and already winter was gone and spring had unfolded. The first lambs and their mothers had arrived in the fields behind her home, and dense clumps of daffodils decorated the front lane.

Contemplating the rippling waters and the still snow-capped peaks beyond, she sighed contentedly, and stretched aching feet – the result of a long walk up the rocky hillside at the back of the house to visit her friend, Sylvie, in her remote farmhouse near the top of the hill that was almost a mountain. *Bloody felt like it too,* she thought. *I'll end up with legs like tree trunks and a belly like Buddha if she keeps feeding me home-made bara brith and Welsh cakes with lashings of butter every time I visit.*

It hadn't been easy at first, meeting new friends and transforming her life, but everything about the move now seemed worth it. She turned from the cottage window to her pet parrot. "It's a bit better than rainy old Manchester, isn't it, Perkins?" But Perkins remained silent, apart from an irritated shake of his wing feathers.

"Are you in a mood, Perkins? You've been very quiet lately. I thought you were doing well with your new Welsh words – even if Old Huw has been teaching you a few phrases I'd rather not know about." The bird remained silent. "Have it your own way – see if I care."

Perkins turned his back and appeared to be closely regarding the far wall.

"Anyway, I'm going to be on Radio Free Gwynedd FM. They want me to talk about my painting, and how I'm fitting into Bala. Maybe they think I'm more interesting than I really am – going to start a hippy nude painting colony or something. Might not be such a bad idea, come to think of it. It would certainly liven things up."

Crystal ignored the silly bird's continued silence and read the letter inviting her onto the mid-morning Chit-Chat programme, broadcast from studios in Barmouth, the next day. It seemed a slot had come up due to the sudden cancellation of fading Welsh celebrity poet, Gruffydd Griffin – 'Gruff Griff' she had read he liked to call himself. She presumed the poet hoped to appeal to a younger audience with the more 'on message' name.

According to the internet page she looked at after going onto Google, Gruff was arrested by police in Aberdovy following a marathon drinking session involving a pint of Welsh moonshine. He had walked naked down the street singing a selection of Manic Street Preacher songs, and compounded his sins by peeing on the bonnet of the first police car that pulled up, and then projectile vomited over three officers. The article said Gruff was now 'resting' at the Priory Clinic south of Manchester.

"You were the only option available at such short notice," the show's producer brightly informed Crystal when she phoned to confirm.

"Thanks. Great honour I'm sure, stepping into the breach, but I can't promise the same fireworks on air as Gruff."

"No. Probably not," admitted the producer. "But it fulfils the 'art' commitment we promised when we won the licence. You'll be fine."

Thanks a lot mate. Just there to meet a quota, concluded Crystal. "Well, if not I suppose you can just stick on another record."

The producer ignored the dig. "Good. That's it then. See you Wednesday, 1pm sharp." He hung up before she could further question him about the show.

* * *

Crystal drove to the coastal resort in the morning, and was now perched in Radio Free Gwynedd's brightly lit front office, being ignored by a receptionist so heavily made-up Crystal thought a geisha would be considered minimalist in comparison. *Poor girl*, she thought. *Probably has a skin condition. A spot of sunlight, and a good splash of soap and water would do her the world of good.*

Music blared loudly from four speakers in the tiny room, in what had obviously once been a shop on the main street. On entering, Crystal noticed that the plastic 'Radio Free Gwynedd – Barmouth Rocks' sign over the doorway had slipped slightly, and the old hoarding was still underneath, offering fish and chips for 2s/6d and a bag of scraps for 6d.

Eventually, the receptionist spared the time between chewing gum, and talking on the phone to someone called Trev – every sentence seeming to end in "totally" – to nod Crystal through to the studios. She was met by an earnest-looking girl, who looked to her to be about twelve years old. "Hi, I'm Sally Evans, and I'll be interviewing you today, mainly about how you come to be here in Wales, and your growing reputation for painting the human form, usually without the benefit of clothes," she added delicately.

"Yes, nudes. It's what I specialise in. I hope I don't mumble, or stutter. I'm not terribly used to being interviewed, particularly live on-air."

"I'm sure you'll be fine. We have more than 500 listeners some days – and that's not including my mum and her friends."

Crystal was led into a small studio – surprised by how scruffy it was. Paper coffee cups strewn everywhere, and bare of furniture apart from a small mixing desk, two microphones and three chairs. One of the chairs was occupied by a solid-looking woman in traditional Welsh dress, with a face Crystal decided resembled a bad-tempered boiled egg. Crystal nodded hello to the woman, who sniffed and looked away. *Must be nervous*, thought Crystal. *Bless.*

Sally donned a pair of headphones and listened intently, raising five fingers to count down to being on-air.

"Hello. Prynhawn da. This is Sally Evans and welcome to Chit-Chat. Today we have Crystal O'Keefe, the celebrated artist, who is making quite a name for herself since emigrating to Wales from Manchester. We also have the celebrated Welsh folk singer, Megan Gwirion, who is going to delight us with a traditional song from her latest album – available exclusively, I might add, on our own Barmouth Rocks label.

"But first we have Crystal. Tell us Crystal why you decided to leave the bright lights of the big city and move to Bala?"

"Well, I moved nine months ago after a failed relationship, and I wanted a total change. My sister, Tish, already lives there, rearing alpacas on a farm up the hillside, and when I visited her I just loved it – the countryside is beautiful and the people I met were really friendly. I bought a cottage by the lakeside and— "

"I believe there's quite a story about the nudes?" interrupted Sally.

"Well… it's how I make my living, but when I arrived I met one of the local characters called Old Huw. He's got a bit of a sense of humour and fed me a line about some Welsh phrases, which, when I tried them out, meant something entirely different. "Ydy pen ol fi yn edrych yn fawr yn hwn?" was one of them, which he told me meant 'Isn't it a fine morning?' It turns out I actually went into a shop and asked 'Does my bum look big in this?' Anyway, I got my revenge by painting a very explicit nude painting of Huw, wrinkles and all, and some very worried looking sheep. I persuaded his local pub to hang it behind the bar, and obviously in a small community people are interested in anything out of the ordinary, and it was certainly that. The reputation I earned from that encounter meant commissions started pouring in. It seems lots of people want a male nude hanging on their wall, so thanks for that Huw."

"And how many of Bala's citizens have you now painted?" asked Sally.

"A couple of dozen men, and so far just a couple of women. It was an unexpected boost to my career, and I'm now getting commissions from further afield. Wrexham seems particularly taken with artistic depictions of the human form."

"And how much do you charge for a painting?"

"I don't tend to discuss prices, except on an individual basis. I had one chap, covered in tattoos almost from head to foot, which makes the painting that much more complicated. And he did have one in a very personal place. I asked him why he had the word 'fog' tattooed there, but when he could see I was interested he… perked up shall we say… and I saw it was actually 'Ffestiniog'. Don't know if I can say this on air at lunchtime, but he said it was because he went like a train. But back to the original question. The charge varies depending on complexity, but I don't charge by the inch." Crystal laughed. "I'll give you a good price if you want one done."

But the joke fell flat as Sally ploughed on, looking at her notes – a blush beginning to light up her freckled cheeks. "And what do you think Megan?"

"It's not a conversation I would wish to have on air thank you very much," pronounced Megan flatly. "I was invited to sing. Is it that time yet?"

"Not quite yet. And is there a man in your life in Wales, Crystal?"

Crystal hesitated. She thought she was going to be asked about art, and had hoped for an opening to talk about her latest idea to move away from nudes to landscapes… but what the hell? "Yes there is actually. I have met a very nice Welsh farmer, David, and I think you could say we are more than just good friends… and there is Old Huw of course. We have now made it up, and he's trying to teach me real Welsh, although he seems to be having more success with my parrot, Perkins, at the moment. I'd like to say he's a father figure to me, but no one deserves a dad like Huw."

Still no reaction. Forget the jokes, decided Crystal.

Sally turned in her chair. "Well, moving on, we have a song now from our celebrated Welsh songstress, Megan. She's just moving to the microphone now. Take it away Megan."

Crystal smiled encouragingly – your turn now – but Megan ignored her, turned to the microphone and began to sing. Her voice rose to a crescendo – managing somehow to be both strident and nasal at the same time, with what to Crystal sounded like gargling coming from somewhere at the back of her throat, which wobbled alarmingly as she 'sang'. Crystal smiled politely, her foot tapping up and down: *God, this is fucking awful. Please let it end and throw a bucket of wine in my direction.*

Eventually it did, and still unsmiling Megan sat down.

"Well, that's all we have time for – so it's goodbye from us, and over to the newsroom for the news where you are," said Sally into the microphone, before flicking a switch.

"Well, that was nice. Thank you," said Crystal politely, and turning to Megan was about to say something encouraging, but the singer swept past muttering incomprehensibly in Welsh.

"I think she was late for another appointment," Sally said apologetically. "Good luck with the painting, and I hope you have every success."

On the way home, Crystal pondered her first experience of radio – something of a let-down. All a bit shallow really, but useful publicity for the painting, she decided.

* * *

Two weeks later and the interview was all but forgotten, as Crystal concentrated on her new ambition – to capture every aspect of the lake's mysterious nature on canvas. Today there was a slight mist, and low cloud delivered a steady drizzle on the slate-grey waters of Llyn Tegid. She set up her easel in the doorway to the wooden artist's studio, built during the winter on the side of her cottage. She was assembling her paints when she glanced up to see a small group of people emerging from the mist on the causeway. All women, they marched purposefully toward the cottage, and Crystal caught what appeared to be hymn singing. *How charming,* she thought. *Some sort of lovely Welsh ceremony, a re-enactment society maybe.* She wondered if they wanted a donation of some sort and reached into the pocket of her paint-stained jeans to find two shiny pound coins.

The group came to a halt outside her cottage and Crystal approached them, smiling.

"Jezebel," shouted one of the group, and another, a stern-looking woman at the back stepped forward. Crystal instantly recognised her – the folk singer from the radio station. "We live clean here in Gwynedd, and don't need the likes of you city people coming down with your wanton ways," Megan stated bluntly. "Buying our homes out from under us, and corrupting our menfolk."

Before Crystal could reply another old codger with thin bandy legs and a whiskery face upbraided her. "Sixty years I've been married, and what my husband has hidden in his trousers remains a mystery to me to this day – one I don't want revealed thank you very much. Never so much as a glimpse at what I've got beneath my winceyette nightie either, I can tell you. Four children we've had, and they were all conceived in the same godly way, with me staring at the ceiling, and him at the pillow. Any hint of a grunt or groan and he was back in the spare bedroom for the night, I can promise you that."

"Well ladies. I'm sorry you feel this way but there's not much I can— "

Crystal was cut off in mid-sentence by another of the women. "The things she must have seen. All those men in all those paintings – it's not right. Everything out on display, like sausages on Mr Jones's slab. If God had meant such things to be seen, he wouldn't have given men trousers. And the men – get all sorts of ideas they will. No decent minded woman will be safe in her bed anymore."

"Come ladies, you know what we have come for." Megan walked to the side of the road with a handful of papers. Another women emerged from the group with a can of lighter fluid and a lighter. "This is what we think of your paintings," said Megan, ripping the papers in half, and throwing them onto the verge.

Crystal peered at the papers littering her verge. "But these aren't my paintings. They appear to be photographs from a magazine called Hustler."

"It's symbolic. Embarrassing to go into my local newsagent in Llanuwchllyn to buy this filth, and very funny looks I got too, but it was worth it." Megan addressed her little congregation, rather than Crystal. With that, the other woman squirted lighter fluid on the pile of photographs and lit them, stepping back sharply as they burst into flames. Another member of the group photographed the ritual burning, on what appeared to be an ancient Kodak Instamatic, before Megan gave Crystal a final self-satisfied "Humphhh", turned on her heel and marched off, with her little band in tow.

Crystal looked down and gasped. "You've burned my *alchemilla mollis* you daft old bats," she shouted at the retreating backs. "And Megan – you sing like a fucking turkey on heat."

The women didn't pause or look round, sturdy backs stiff in righteousness, as they marched off like stormtroopers in drag, and soon were lost in mist on the causeway.

Crystal was stunned – so far she had received nothing but welcome from her neighbours. *I must phone David, see what he makes of it,* she thought. Stepping inside the house she saw Perkins' cage door was ajar – it must have been left open after the bird's daily flutter.

The cage was empty, and she looked around the room to see Perkins standing on the ledge of an open window. "There you are, Perkins. Come to Mummy."

But Perkins had other ideas. He turned to Crystal and squawked what sounded to her very much like 'Uhuru', before launching himself through the window, and away in a flutter of wings.

Crystal ran to the window, but couldn't see him anywhere. She rushed to the door, and scanned the surrounding trees – nothing. "You stupid, stupid bird. You can't survive out there on your own. PERKINS," she shouted, but if the bird could hear he didn't respond. Through all her troubles, her foul-mouthed pet had been the only constant in her life. Suddenly, she couldn't imagine life without him.

Reluctantly, Crystal went inside and reached for the phone. "David? Are you busy at the moment? I need a bit of help."

"Are you all right? You sound a bit shaky."

The pressures of the day finally hit Crystal, and on hearing David's voice she burst into floods of tears. "I'll be right over. Ten minutes."

* * *

Crystal had calmed down by the time David arrived, screeching into her drive with a spray of gravel from the tyres on his Ford pick-up. "Sorry about that. Not usually the tearful sort – usually just get on with things – but today's been an absolute bastard."

She related the events of the day – starting with her encounter with Megan and ending with Perkins' escape into the countryside.

David shrugged his shoulders. "Not much we can do about Perkins. Ask people to keep an eye out for him. We can put it on Bala Online and hope he gets spotted, or he may just come back when he gets hungry. He's a clever bird that one, so I wouldn't be at all surprised if he didn't just turn up one day. As for the old battleaxes, I have an idea who they may be. Can I use your laptop?"

After tapping on the keyboard for a couple of minutes, David gave a satisfied "Hmmmmm… " and put the laptop to one side. "What you have come up against is an organisation called Merched y Mynyddoedd – Women of the Mountains – sort of nutty Presbyterian version of the Taliban. They once accused the Archbishop of Wales of being under satanic influence for speaking out in support of human rights for illegal immigrants. To them that's a category that should include you, being from over the border in England. Your folk singer, Megan, is the leading light of the group.

"Apparently, they believe in a sort of idealised Wales that went out hundreds of years ago – if it ever existed. You're probably lucky they didn't bring a ducking stool with them, or you would've been in the lake by now. Don't like outsiders, and particularly don't like the English.

"I wouldn't take them too seriously though. They don't have much influence in a place like Bala. Most people here depend on visitors in one way or the other. Bit more of a stronghold for them in the villages further up the valley though."

Crystal left David's side and paced the room. "But I do care, David. I didn't come here to be accosted outside my own home, and have nutty fundamentalists burning plants I brought all the way from Manchester. I thought I'd moved to Wales – not Afghanistan or the bloody Swat Valley. Don't worry, I'll think of something."

Smiling now, as David's presence lightened her black mood a little, she reached for his hand. "In the meantime, I think I need consoling with a stiff gin and tonic… and later a bit of mortal sin wouldn't be totally out of the question… "

* * *

It was a week later when Crystal heard her local free newspaper drop through the door. It usually went straight into the recycle bin, but the first thing Crystal noticed was her picture on the front page, looking aghast as the Women of the Mountains torched her favourite plant. Megan had a particularly smug look on her face. Above the picture was the headline "English Nude 'Artist' Gets Stark Warning", and below an interview with Megan, about how the immoral English were taking over the area. It quoted her saying, "I walk down the high street nowadays, and hear not one word of Welsh spoken. It makes me feel very uncomfortable. We Welsh people should stand up and say enough is enough. We can't have this uncontrolled immigration of people whose lifestyle is alien to us."

Bloody cheek, thought Crystal. *What happened to my right of reply?*

Scanning the paper, she saw a telephone number for editorial in Chester. So much for Wales! She rang the number. A disinterested-sounding nasal female voice answered: "Hello. Wales and West of England News Group. Can I help you?"

"Hello, I've just been reading the Bala and Llanuwchllyn Weekly News, and you have a story and picture about me on the front page— "

"Hold on. Putting you through," said the receptionist – cutting Crystal off in mid-sentence.

A click, and a male voice came on the phone. Still English. "Hello, reporters here. What can I do for you?"

Crystal explained who she was and asked, her voice rising with her anger, "Why didn't you call me for my side of the story? I'm in the phone book and even have a website – all someone had to do was pick up a phone, and I would certainly have had something to say about the implication that I am immoral, some sort of harlot… not godly enough for Wales.

"I must say, I haven't seen many of my Welsh friends beating a path to the church door come Sunday. The Glyndwr Arms more likely."

"Look, I'm sorry. I didn't write the story," said the reporter. "I'm guessing that there wasn't time to get in touch with you, but we would certainly be happy to interview you for the next edition.

Why don't I get the local chap who wrote the story to ring you? We produce a dozen editions of local papers here you see. Same adverts, and most of the same stories in them all, and just the front page and local sport is changed, depending where you are."

Crystal wasn't sure she could trust the local stringer to put her side of the argument. "Give me his name and number, and perhaps I'll ring him later in the week."

Putting the phone down, she muttered to herself. "Right, Megan Gwirion. Let's see what we can find out about you."

She typed Megan's name into Google and came up with a dozen websites which mentioned her. Most giving bare details about her folk singing career, which appeared to have peaked as a member of a choir competing at the Junior Eisteddfod in 1979. Her membership of Women of the Mountains was more prominent, with mention of various protest events in which she had been involved – campaigns to have Welsh-only signs in Snowdonia, the banning of any ethnic food restaurants within the National Park, and the raising of a Welsh Militia to man the borders. One website caught her eye, www.folksingersinwales with photographs and autobiographical details of various musicians.

Megan was mentioned, and the site said she was brought up on a farm near a small village on Anglesey, near Amlwch. None of the other websites mentioned this, Crystal noted. Might be worth checking out, and she had never been to Anglesey.

The next day she got into her little Honda Jazz to make the 65-mile journey, taking a few sandwiches and a bottle of water in case she got peckish on the way. Before leaving, she looked into the trees, hoping to catch sight of Perkins. He hadn't been spotted since flying out of the window a week before, and today was no different. She sighed resignedly, and got into her car, driving across the causeway and onto the A4212. *Even if this gets me nowhere, it's a lovely drive across Snowdonia*, thought Crystal. *Must be careful about the speed traps* – she had read they were everywhere on that road. She drove extra carefully, the road passing over mountains, and through forests, until the landscape finally became gentler as she neared Anglesey, and travelled over the Menai Bridge and north to Amlwch.

About 10 miles from the resort, Crystal arrived in the small village mentioned on the website. Spotting a shop, she pulled up. This would be a good place to start – fount of all local knowledge, shopkeepers. She looked at herself in the car mirror – her mass of red curls particularly wild today, and wearing jeans and a kaftan. Yes, she'd pass off as a folky type. On opening the shop door a bell tinkled – a little like stepping back into the 1930s. Behind the counter stood a frail old lady, with wispy white hair and what looked like seriously crossed eyes. Another customer was already in the shop, eyeing cans of corned beef, baked beans and Wonderloaf. There didn't seem to be much else on sale, apart from milk and butter in an old open fridge which hummed noisily in the corner, though Crystal thought she caught a whiff of paraffin in the air.

The woman behind the counter looked directly toward her. "Can I help you?"

"Yes… " began Crystal – but while still apparently looking at her the shopkeeper pointed to the other customer. "No, I mean you."

Oh God, thought Crystal. *This is going to be difficult.*

"You're all right luv," said the other customer. "I've not quite decided yet. Go ahead."

Decided, thought Crystal – *not a hard fuckin' choice. Corn beef sandwich or baked beans on toast.* "Thanks," she said, turning to the shopkeeper. "Hi. I'm a music journalist, and I'm researching a piece about the folk singer, Megan Gwirion. I believe she used to live here in the village."

The shopkeeper looked nonplussed, her eyes scanning the shop like a scattergun on automatic. "Not sure I can think of anyone by that name… no… but come to think of it, you may be thinking of little Mavis. She did change her name to something like what you said, when she started singing. Mavis Daft – not the prettiest girl in the world – and the name wouldn't help. Family had the farm up the road, but didn't mix much. Kept themselves to themselves you might say. Thought they were a cut above if you ask me."

"How do I get there?" asked Crystal.

"Can't miss it. White building about half a mile out of the village if you follow the road through. Not been a farm since they bought it though. I'm not sure anyone there would remember them now – they moved back to Somerset I believe."

"How do you mean, moved back?" asked Crystal.

"Well, that's where they came from, when Mavis was a little girl. Face like a boiled egg I always thought. Now, can I help you if you're ready?" she said, turning her attention to apparently peer at the Wonderloaf shelf, as the other customer approached the counter holding a can of beans.

* * *

"Megan, you hypocritical old cow," muttered Crystal to herself, as she drove to the farmhouse. "Not even originally from Wales."

The shopkeeper had described the farm's location accurately – a neat two-storey building set back from the road, with a farm gate leading into an ornate garden. The smell of roses hung sweetly in the still, warm air, as Crystal undid the latch and walked up the drive past neat flower beds – giving the knocker a firm rap when she reached the door. She heard movement inside and the sound of bolts being drawn back. The door opened with a slight creak.

Crystal peered into the gloomy hallway, to see an elderly man dressed like he had stolen his clothes from a scarecrow – a ripped checked shirt, and ancient corduroys that had lost most of their cord. "Sorry about the appearance. Been gardening don't you know," the man said, in an accent that sounded like he was auditioning for a part in Jeeves and Wooster.

"Hello. I wonder if you can help me? I'm a music journalist, and I'm researching for a feature about the folk singer, Megan Gwirion. The shopkeeper in the village said she used to live here?"

"Sold me the house, actually. Names Gerald, by the way. Gerald Pettigrew-Soames. Retired down here about ten years ago. Lucky to get the place actually. Come in and have a cup of tea, and I'll explain. Don't get a lot of company out here, so it's nice to have a visitor now and then."

Five minutes later and Crystal sat in an ancient armchair, balancing a cup of tea and dainty cake on her knee. She was being treated to Gerald's life history. "Twenty years in the army. Guards. Then another ten in the City. Merchant bank." Crystal was by now getting used to his staccato delivery. Years in the army shouting orders, she presumed.

"Met Megan. Mavis. Whatever. Anyway, upshot was the house had already gone. Young local couple with a baby had offered full asking price. Peanuts to me, so upped it by £5,000. Felt a bit guilty, truth to tell, but all's fair in love, war and buying houses eh?

"Anyway, whatshername jumped at the chance of some more dosh, and told the young couple where to get off. Lived here ever since."

"You are sure it was Megan who sold you the house, not her parents?" asked Crystal.

"Yep. Quite sure. Her name on the deeds. Original name. Daft by name, but not by nature eh? Megan was the stage name she was using then. I remember her telling me that. Got the deeds somewhere if you'd care to look? Believe the parents had died, and she was using the place as a holiday cottage – getting a pretty penny for it as well, but she must have wanted to get her hands on the main loot. House had shot up in price you see."

Crystal asked a few more questions to make her cover story credible, but Gerald didn't know any more about Megan – not that it mattered. Crystal had everything she needed. Don't get mad. Time to get even.

* * *

Back home, Crystal pondered what she should do next. She had enough on Megan to ruin her reputation as a Welsh firebrand, but how should she use it? Go straight to the local newspaper, and expose Megan for what she was – an English incomer, who happily gazumped a Welsh couple to sell her holiday let to an English toff!

No, she decided. This would end where it started. At Radio Free Gwynedd.

She reached for her contact book and dialled the number in Barmouth. "Hello. Is Sally Evans there? It's Crystal O'Keefe wanting to speak to her. I was on the show a little while ago. Thanks, I'll hold."

Crystal waited for a minute, listening idly to the background chatter in the studio, and the muffled sound of music. Finally, the phone was lifted. "Hi. It's Sally here. What can I do for you, Crystal?"

"I don't know if you've been keeping up with the local news," said Crystal. "But I've been getting a bit of unwanted publicity from Merched y Mynyddoedd – the Women of the Mountains – and in particular from Megan Gwirion, who I was on the show with."

There was a slight pause on the line. "Yes, I did hear something about that." Sally sounded defensive. "We can't be held responsible for anything that happens outside the studio you know."

"Of course not," said Crystal. "But I have a proposition for you. I thought it might make an interesting show to get us both back on, to debate the issues – English people moving to Wales, and what effect it's having on local society – what the pros and cons are, that sort of thing. What do you think?"

Sally sounded enthusiastic. "It could be really good. I don't know if Megan would go for it mind you – but in principle I think it's a great idea."

"She seemed pretty happy to stand outside my house giving her point of view, and to speak to the local papers, so I can't see why she wouldn't take the opportunity to have another go at me," said Crystal. "It has to be Megan though – otherwise I'm not interested."

"Leave it with me," replied Sally. "I'll get back to you."

Crystal put the phone down with a satisfied smile. *Let's just hope Megan takes the bait, and I get to reel the old trout in.* It wasn't a long wait. Within the hour the phone rang and Crystal answered: "Hello. Hi Sally. Next Tuesday? That would be great. Lunchtime show sounds good to me. Believe me, I'm looking forward to it. See you then."

Crystal put the phone down, thought for a moment, and picked it up again, dialling the number she had been given by the news reporter in Chester. The phone was answered by an elderly-sounding man with lilting Welsh. "Bore da. Gallaf eich helpu chi?"

"Hello," said Crystal. "I've been given your number by the newsroom in Chester. I believe you're the local reporter for the Bala and Llanuwchllyn Weekly News?"

"Yes. Colin Matthews is the name. How can I help you?"

"I think you spoke to Megan Gwirion about me a few weeks ago. I'm the artist who paints nudes. Remember me? You put me on the front page."

"I do remember, and the news editor in Chester has spoken to me about you – said I might expect a call," replied the reporter carefully. "I did mean to contact you, but the edition was about to go. Do you want to give me your reaction now?"

"No," said Crystal. "I'm just ringing to tell you that Megan and I will be coming face-to-face on Radio Free Gwynedd, at lunchtime next Tuesday, on Chit-Chat. It could be well worth your while listening – and I'll take that as my right to reply. OK?"

"Thanks. I promise to listen to the show. What line are you going to take?"

"I'm afraid I'm not saying anything else at the moment. You'll just have to listen. Got to go now, but I might be available to talk after the show. Goodbye."

* * *

Crystal got up early on Tuesday, to get ready to travel to Barmouth. Spot of lippy, lucky knickers on, easy on the coffee – don't want to be going to the toilet halfway through! She felt nervous, but ready to join battle with the dreadful Megan. *Must be the fighting Irish in me.* Still no sign of Perkins though. She put extra bird seed out, including some of his favourite treats, in the hope of enticing him back, but there were still no sightings. Maybe one day he would turn up?

The journey across to Barmouth was uneventful, and Crystal whiled away half an hour watching the waves crash to shore, before walking into the studio.

Geisha girl was still in post behind the reception desk, and Crystal noticed that despite the half-an-inch of slap on her face, her fingers were small and dumpy, with badly chewed nails and what looked like a self-inflicted tattoo in the shape of a star on the base of her thumb. Somewhere underneath all that make-up was a young girl, probably not long out of school, trying to make her way in a big bad world, she realised – and started to understand the girl a little better. Didn't make her any more polite though. Words emanated from the plaster-doll face. "Waiting for you. You know where you're going – same place as before."

"Thanks," said Crystal, walking through the doors to the studio.

Sally was waiting for her, along with two other people – Megan, who eyed her like a buzzard might regard a tasty field mouse, and a skinny middle-aged man in faded jeans, with long hair tied in a ponytail. He had one of those faces that looked like someone you knew, but couldn't quite place – like a rock star from long ago, who had once been handsome in a young Keith Richards sort of way.

"Hello," said Sally. "Megan you already know, and I hope you don't mind, but we asked Gruffydd Griffin to join us. He was supposed to be on before, if you remember, and we'd already paid him, so he's joining us today for the discussion."

"Hello Gruff." Crystal extended her hand. "Pleased to meet you. Hope you're feeling better."

"Fine, thank you," said Gruff, shaking her hand with a smile. "Never better. Listened to the last show, just to bring me up to speed with what we're talking about. Liked the joke about Ffestiniog – it inspired me to write a little poem. Matter of fact I'm using it in the live stage show, so thanks for the inspiration."

He looked her slowly up and down, from the mass of curly red hair to Converse baseball boots. "Might write a poem about you if I get the muse. Just need to think of a word that rhymes with shaggable."

"I'll take that as a compliment," said Crystal lightly. "After the show you might want to think of something that rhymes with 'kick in the nuts'."

"God, I bloody like her," exclaimed Gruff to no one in particular. "What do you think Megan love? She's a card isn't she?"

Megan regarded him with no attempt to disguise her contempt. "Let's just get on with it shall we? I'll say what I want to say when the show starts."

Sally sat them down, and started her preamble. "If you've been listening to the news, we had Megan and Crystal on a few weeks back, and the show started a bit of a controversy. Megan, who believes in all things Welsh, took exception to Crystal moving to Bala, and starting a business specialising in painting local men in the nude— "

Megan cut in: "I think my group and I have every right to express our opinion that there is no place in this part of Wales for people like her. They come here, buying up properties that should be reserved for Welsh people, and bring with them ideas that I can only describe as corrupting to our way of life."

Crystal replied sharply, "Before I bought my cottage there wasn't a queue of Welsh people lining up to buy it, and it had been on the market for nearly a year – fact is the estate agent nearly bit my hand off when I offered a good price. And presumably it was a Welsh person who sold it to me."

Gruff roused himself from what appeared to be a deep sleep, and interjected: "Maybe Megan wants to reserve homes for all those millions of Jones's and Evans's who are living in Birmingham, Manchester and London now – just in case they decide it's all been a terrible mistake, moving to England, and want to come home."

"What do you say to that, Megan?" asked Sally.

"I say that it doesn't really matter what happens in England – or Cardiff, or Swansea where Mr Griffin comes from for that matter. But in the heart of the National Park in Snowdonia it is God's own country and should be reserved for God's own people – the Welsh. Our homeland if you like."

Sally turned to Crystal. "What do you say about that, Crystal? Does she have a point?"

Time to lance the dragon. "You know Megan, or should I call you Mavis, I would take what you say seriously if it wasn't for the fact that you are a total hypocrite."

Megan's mouth opened and closed, but no words emanated. Gruff looked wide awake now. His poet's nose smelled blood in the water, and he could sense a shark circling for the kill. "Fact is, Megan, you yourself gazumped a lovely Welsh couple with a baby, to sell your holiday home on Anglesey to a rich Englishman. Mind you, it wouldn't really matter to you, given that just like me you are in fact English yourself by birth, even if you have adopted Wales as your homeland – just as I wish to do." Crystal dug into her pocket to pull out a piece of paper.

"I have a copy of your birth certificate from the Register Office in Weston-super-Mare. Your birth name was Mavis Daft, born in Somerset in 1963. Is that not correct Mavis? Here you are, you can get your friends to burn that." Crystal reached to hand over the certificate.

Megan didn't answer or take the document, but her face was bright red as she stormed out of the studio, slamming the door as she left. "Blimey, she was a bit shirty," remarked Gruff, looking admiringly towards Crystal.

"Well," piped up Sally. "We certainly promised you a lively debate, and it seems we have made some more news – you heard it first on Radio Free Gwynned. Now, let's have some music... and a poem from Gruff. Not the one about the prick... sorry... penis... you know the one I mean. Sorry Mum."

* * *

Back home several days later, Crystal smiled – a bit smugly, she guiltily admitted to herself – as she scanned the local newspaper. On the front page a picture of Megan, attacking a journalist with an antique bedpan outside her home. More reporters and cameramen were pictured camped in her garden. She read that following the media scrum the house in Llanuwchllyn was now empty, and no one had seen Megan since that day. *Brought it on yourself, you old bat*, thought Crystal. *I don't feel any sympathy – well, maybe a tiny bit.*

Glancing out of the back window she saw two large crows on the bird table. Bit unusual. Stepping out into the garden she thought they were maybe after Perkins' special treats.

The crows didn't seem perturbed by her presence, and as she approached one of them regarded her with a beady eye: "Who's a twat?" it asked before they both flew off with lazy beats of their wings.

Crystal was dumbfounded. *Perkins. You are out there somewhere – and still alive.*

PERKINS' STORY

The phone was ringing when Crystal returned to the cottage from a shopping expedition to Wrexham with Sylvie. She had just dropped her friend off at the remote farmhouse on the hillside south of Lake Bala before returning home, and heard the phone as she struggled at the door, balancing shopping bags in one hand while she turned the key in the lock with the other. By the time she got the door open, and the burglar alarm turned off, the phone had stopped. A minute later the message display bleeped. Crystal pushed the listen button and found the call had been from best pal, Freddie, from Manchester: "Coming round this afto if that's OK? Bringing my niece Sally, and a friend. 'Bout three. Bye."

It struck Crystal this was uncharacteristically brief for Freddie. She hadn't even asked her to ring back. Freddie usually rang and chatted for at least half an hour, even if they were soon to meet. Intriguing.

She looked at her watch – already past midday – better get something ready to eat for when they arrive. *Lucky I've just been shopping*, she thought. *Sorry, David. That's your crumpets gone for a Burton!*

Crystal had just put the finishing touches to what she considered a fine Welsh afternoon tea, when she heard the familiar burble of the ancient Mercedes' V8 engine that signalled Freddie's arrival with mystery guest. Freddie's husband Nigel had insisted on keeping the German limousine as the family car, despite its size and impracticality. It swept into the driveway with a crunch of gravel and stopped.

Crystal waved out of the window as Freddie stepped out of the massive vehicle. From the passenger side a young girl aged about twelve emerged, blonde plaits swaying. She looked tiny against the polished silver edifice of the car. The girl opened the rear passenger door – and out jumped a sleek brindle-coloured greyhound, its nose twitching at unfamiliar scents.

The car's arrival caused a stir in the field adjoining Crystal's cottage, and Skippy trotted to the fence to see what was going on – Freddie usually fed him with his favourite treats when she visited, and he always came to greet her in the hope of some food.

Spotting Skippy, the dog walked to the fence – poking his long nose through the wire. The two cautiously inspected each other, and decided they liked what they saw and smelled, because the dog licked Skippy's nose, and the sheep baaad with pleasure.

"He's very gentle," the girl explained to Crystal. "He's called Ben, and used to be a racer called Brown Bomber. My name's Sally, by the way," she extended her hand to Crystal. "I'm very pleased to meet you."

"Pleased to meet you too," said Crystal – *how grown-up the girl seemed.*

"To what do we owe the pleasure of this visit?" Crystal asked, turning to Freddie. "You're very welcome of course, but usually I have a bit more notice. You mentioned Sally, and a friend. Would that friend be Ben by any chance?"

Freddie gave her a guilty look. "We have a favour to ask – and it's a big one. Can we go inside?"

Ben left his new-found friend, casting a reluctant glance over his shoulder at Skippy, and on long springy legs followed the others into the cottage to sit on the rug in front of the log-burning stove, settling down as if the house was already familiar territory.

Sally took charge as soon as they got inside. "The thing is, Ben's been a big part of our family for several years – since soon after my mum died. Dad thought he'd got a dog for me, but the truth is I wanted him to keep my dad company – he works from home a lot, and seemed terribly lonely after Mum died."

"It was cancer," said Freddie, taking up the story. "I don't think you knew Sally's mum. We weren't that close as a family, but we kept in touch and I always went to Sally's birthday parties."

"Anyway," said Sally. "The point is that Dad's been offered a new job. It's a great opportunity, but it's in the Middle East, and we can't take Ben with us. He's more than just a dog to us because a few years ago he saved Dad from being attacked by a mugger with a knife, and he nearly died doing it. Trouble was the man had a Rottweiler with him and he savaged Ben. He nearly lost one of his back legs, but managed to run for help and saved Dad from being really badly hurt – or worse."

"I'd have him, but we live in a flat in the city centre, and we're not allowed dogs," said Freddie. "Anyway, it just wouldn't be practical."

Ben roused himself from the fireside and put his head on Crystal's lap, fixing her with big brown eyes that seemed to look right into her heart – *talk about a stitch-up*, thought Crystal.

"When Auntie Frederica told me about you living in this lovely part of the country, and what a kind person you were, I knew I had the answer. Ben could stay here with you, and I know he'd make you happy too. I love Ben, and can't think of any other answer to the problem. I couldn't stand it if I thought he would be sad with someone who wouldn't look after him properly. Please," she implored. "Say you'll take him in."

"I don't know," said Crystal. "I'm not sure I'm a doggy sort of person, and what would happen if he chased sheep? Farmers round here shoot dogs if they worry sheep, you know."

"You saw how he was with that big funny-looking sheep with the wrinkly nose," said Sally. "He doesn't have a horrible bone in his body, and he's very clever. He can do tricks too, and smell anything out once he gets the scent. Sometimes I think he understands every word I say— "

"How long do I have to think about it?" interrupted Crystal.

"We fly to Dubai in two days. I was rather hoping we could leave him here. I've got his bowls and his favourite blanket in the car, and lots and lots of food, which should keep him going for quite a while. Please. I don't know where else to turn." Three sets of eyes fixed on Crystal. Done up like a kipper, she realised.

"All right," said Crystal reluctantly. "But any problems at all, and I hand him right back to Freddie. OK? And don't think I won't. This is very much a trial." She fixed Freddie with an 'I really mean it' stare.

"There won't be a problem," promised Sally, her bright blue eyes brimming with tears. "I just know you are going to love each other, and be great friends. I wouldn't leave him with anyone if there was any other way."

Sally hugged Ben as she left, tears still in her eyes, and whispered something in his ear. The dog whimpered slightly as Sally climbed into the big old Mercedes, but stayed at Crystal's side as the big car backed down the drive, and turned over the bridge on the road back to Manchester. She felt the warmth of his body against her leg, and felt his breathing, as she waved Freddie and Sally goodbye. As she looked down, Ben looked up at her, then loped inside to flop back in front of the stove. "You are one clever dog," said Crystal. "Welcome to the family."

* * *

David visited that night, and Crystal met him at the door. "I have a bit of a surprise for you. You'll never guess."

"I already have – you've got a dog here," said David.

"How did you know that?" Crystal asked, genuinely surprised at David's feat of second sight.

"Not difficult. He's standing beside you. Hello boy, how are you?"

Ben had arrived at her side, silent as a ghost, and gave a good-natured growl of pleasure as David roughly tickled his ears with big rough farmer's hands which looked massive against the greyhound's sleek head.

David stepped into the room with Ben at his side. "Who are you dog-sitting for? I don't know anyone from round here with a greyhound, though I've seen a few knocking round the estate. Not like this one though – more like lurchers usually. They use them for hunting rabbits and that sort of thing."

"There isn't anyone," replied Crystal. "It seems I've sort of acquired him. I'll tell you all about it over a glass of wine or three."

They sat together on the sofa and as David reached over to embrace Crystal the dog jumped between them, nuzzling Crystal and trying to push David to one side. "I understand dogs, and what he's trying to do is protect you, and assert himself as the boss at the same time." David shoved the dog off the sofa. "Sit," he commanded, and reluctantly Ben returned to his place by the stove, where his favourite blanket had been spread, but continued looking at the two of them with jealous eyes.

"We've had dogs all my life," said David. "They aren't let into the house, mind. Working dogs that have to earn their living. You know you're going to have to exercise this one every day? Long walks even if the weather's bad. And you need to keep him well away from sheep…"

"I know," said Crystal. "We've already been through that. Apparently, he won't chase sheep, and he's already made friends with Skippy. Might go after the odd rabbit or hare given his training at the dog track, mind you. Could provide a meal or two for the slow cooker with a bit of luck. Anyway, let's go to bed – not you, Ben. Stay." The dog made a move to go upstairs with them, but reluctantly settled back down in front of the fire again, with a distinct "humph" of disappointment.

* * *

Over the coming weeks the two of them relaxed into a routine – long walks in the morning, with Ben loping at Crystal's side, occasionally running off to investigate a new smell that interested him. But he always came back when called, and showed only passing interest in the sheep in the fields, despite his continued infatuation with Skippy. Sally had been right – he seemed to instinctively know what he could do, and what was off limits.

In the afternoon Crystal took her sketch book, and set off with Ben to try and find another aspect of Llyn Tegid that it had not yet revealed to her, a different viewpoint, or another facet of the lake's illusive character. Today, the lake was placid, the surrounding mountains reflected in the slate-grey water. Ben sat patiently by her side panting, steam showing on his breath. It was early summer, but still cool on the hillsides. She sketched, and this time included Ben in the landscape. His brindle coat blended into the bracken, which was still brown from winter but with new green shoots beginning to show through in sunnier spots. She decided she would turn it into a full watercolour painting, and send it to Sally as a present. Sally could put it on the wall of her new home in Dubai to remind her of Ben.

Later, as they walked down the hill, she sensed Ben was keen to get home, running forward and then back, frustrated by Crystal's slow pace. "Take it easy, Ben. I don't have long legs like you, and I'm pulling a bit more weight."

As they turned into the drive, she instantly saw what had urged Ben forward. Ted, the farmer, was in the field, herding some of the sheep into a cattle truck, and Ben vaulted the fence to stand with Skippy. "Hello, Crystal," Ted greeted. "Just taking some of the sheep over to another field – should be in lamb now, and I want to make some room here for when they all arrive. Just hope Skippy's been doing his job."

Wouldn't count on it, thought Crystal, but said nothing. The ram seemed more interested in his new friend than the sheep, though she had seen him occasionally performing his duty when Ben wasn't around to amuse him.

As the summer stretched out, the dog's friendship with Skippy continued unabated. The two were constant companions, sitting side-by-side, and rolling on the ground together, the other sheep looking on in bemusement. "You are a very odd couple," remarked Crystal, as the two of them stood by the fence. "You are supposed to be servicing the lady sheep that have been put in the field for you, Skippy. And you," she said, turning to Ben. "You are supposed to be doing doggy things like licking your privates, and barking at strangers. This is becoming a very strange household. Mad dog, Englishwoman and a daft Welsh ram – no midday sun at the moment though." She looked up at the overcast sky, and they looked at Crystal like she was intruding on their private space, before turning their backs and running to a far corner of the field.

True to her word, Sally emailed regularly. Her dad's job was going well, and she was settling into the English school in Dubai. She wrote that she missed Ben, but Crystal told her there was no problem – she and Ben were getting along just fine, and he had made a friend – if a rather odd one for a dog.

Crystal now knew when David was about to arrive – Ben would run to the door five minutes before his car drew in and sit there, tail wagging in anticipation. She had no idea how the dog performed this trick – magnificent hearing, smell, or some canine second sight. She preferred to think it might be the latter, but their party trick was to have the tea brewed, or a glass of wine poured, before he arrived. "You must have heard me coming," David often remarked, as Crystal and Ben exchanged glances.

Ben's other remarkable gifts would soon become apparent.

* * *

Crystal and Ben had just returned from their morning walk through the light rain of a typical Welsh summer. He had been dried off and was stretched out on his blanket and Crystal was in the kitchen making a batch of bara brith, her hands caked in flour and egg mix, when she heard a light tap at the door. Stretching to the window she looked out – but no one was there.

Ben was on his feet, sniffing at the bottom of the door, and looking at her – but she shrugged: "No one there, Ben. Must have been the wind knocking a twig against the door, or something."

Ben didn't look convinced. He went back to sit on his blanket, but his nose and ears were twitching and he continued to look at the door, as if he sensed there was something, or someone, outside.

Crystal was about to put her cake into the oven when she heard the tap again. This was very strange. She looked again… and again nothing… but this time Ben was on his feet, and whining to be let out.

"Want to spend a penny?" said Crystal, opening the door. "There you go."

Ben shot out of the door, and appeared to be taking great interest in a pile of leaves that had accumulated between the back door and the entrance to the studio. She heard the dog snuffling about, and turned back to her cake – this time popping it into the oven.

Ben appeared in the doorway holding something in his jaws. "What have you got there, Ben? Nothing horrible I hope – no, don't bring it into the house."

But Ben ignored her, and came into the kitchen, to delicately place his find in front of Crystal and back off, barking. He never barked, thought Crystal, and looked at what appeared to be a bedraggled dead bird on the floor. Then she saw a flash of blue and green on the feathers, and looked again.

"Perkins," she gasped, her hand flying to her mouth. "Is it really you?"

Crystal picked up Perkins – he was still warm, and she felt a faint heartbeat.

She got kitchen roll, and gently dried Perkins' feathers, and sat in front of the stove with him in her lap – he lay still, but she could feel he was alive. "Thank you Ben. It must have been Perkins we heard at the door, trying to get in. You may have saved his life – if he pulls through that is. It doesn't look promising, but we'll keep him warm and pray he comes round."

Crystal wondered if she should take Perkins to the local vet, but decided he was probably too weak – moving him further may kill him. So she turned the oven off, leaving the half-baked bara brith inside, and the hours passed. She sat in front of the stove, the tick of a clock the only sound, as day gave way to evening, and the cottage interior grew dark.

She snoozed on-and-off and Ben curled in front of the stove, his back legs occasionally twitching, and the occasional yelp and a low growl escaping from his muzzle – Crystal supposed he was having doggie dreams, chasing rabbits or more likely playing in the field with Skippy.

The phone rang once, but she ignored it and let it click onto message. "Hello, it's David here. Can't come over tonight, we have a cow in labour and it looks like it's going to be complicated. The vet's on the way, but I've no idea when we're going to be finished. Ring you tomorrow. Bye… "

At last she had to admit, she needed to go to the lavvy – absolutely bursting. She rose, stiff from hours of inactivity, and carefully placed Perkins on a chair cushion, before heading upstairs for a much needed comfort break. "God, I needed that," she pronounced to no one in particular, as she headed back down the stairs.

In the front room, Ben had also woken from his slumbers, and was gently nuzzling Perkins, snuffling and making odd whimpering noises. "Leave him be, Ben," said Crystal. "I know you're trying to help, but— " She was interrupted when Ben stepped back with a loud bark – and Perkins replied with a faint squawk, and attempted to struggle to his feet.

"Perkins – you're back," said Crystal. "Thanks, Ben. I don't know what you just did, but it seemed to work."

Perkins was up on his feet, but stumbling round like a drunken man – it reminded Crystal of Old Huw when he had taken a few too many sips from his hip flask at the Bala's Got Talent contest, and after the competition she'd had to ring his son, Gandalf, to take him home from the pub.

Crystal had virtually given Perkins up for lost months ago, but had kept his dried treats just in case, and now rushed to get them from the back of the grocery shelf. "Here, Perkins. Try one of these," she said, offering him a piece of dried food from the Pretty Bird packet. Perkins took the offering and swallowed it in one, emitting a harsh squawk. She continued to feed him, until he pushed the proffered morsel away with his beak, stretched his wings and let fly with another haunting cry. It suddenly dawned on Crystal: "You're speaking crow! You must have been living among them so long, you've forgotten your English and Welsh words. Never mind Perkins, I'm sure it'll all come back to you in time. Old Huw will soon get you remembering some of his silly old phrases. Remind me to look up 'Ti'n Goc Oen' one day, and see what it means – it certainly made David laugh when you used to come out with it, but he never told me what it meant – just said 'you probably don't want to know.'"

* * *

Perkins' recovery continued, and the next day Crystal took him to the local vet, where he managed to draw blood as the young medic's hand got a bit too close to his beak. "Little bugger!" he yelped, withdrawing his hand. "Sorry. Very unprofessional – he just caught me by surprise. Doesn't seem a lot wrong with him – he's certainly rather feisty today. I'd say keep him warm and keep an eye on him for a few more days. Any problems just ring the surgery. He's lucky to have survived outdoors in the weather we've had during the winter – bit of a miracle, actually. See the receptionist outside, she'll sort out the bill with you."

Crystal put Perkins back in his cage, and the bird regarded her with a beady eye. "You're a naughty boy, Perkins, pecking the nice young man. Thanks." She extended her hand to the young vet – only to quickly snatch it back when she glanced at the bloody mess that was offered in return, hastily patched up with tissues. "Yes, well thanks again – sorry about the… er… damage to your hand."

Crystal walked back to her little Honda Jazz, parked on the road, muttering to herself, "Forty bloody quid. We were only in there for ten minutes. I'd have given him a nip myself if I'd known he was going to charge that much." Ben was curled up in the back seat, but jumped up when he spotted Crystal and stuck his head between the two front seats, tail wagging, as Crystal loaded Perkins' cage into the front, and secured it with the seat belt. Perkins disdainfully ignored the dog and looked away, his hooked beak in the air – a patrician lord to whom this lowly subject was not worthy of attention.

Ben didn't seem to mind, and settled back into the seat for the ten-minute journey to the cottage, but rose, wagging his tail, as they pulled into the drive. "I know what you want, Ben. OK, go and say hello." The dog leapt out of the car, and in a single bound cleared the field fence and ran to where Skippy was 'pleasuring' one of the sheep, which seemed to take only a few seconds before he was finished. Skippy walked over to where Ben waited, with a shake of his shaggy coat and what to Crystal looked like a definite swagger – Liam Gallagher with grey dreadlocks.

Crystal walked to the cottage carrying Perkins' cage, and opened the door for the bird's daily flutter – first making sure all the windows were shut.

Perkins hopped out and managed a half-hearted flight round the room, before alighting on the window sill, where he stood looking out, emitting a series of crow-like caws. "I think I preferred the swear words, Perkins. I'm just going to make myself coffee and read the morning paper – see you in ten minutes."

The cawing continued while Crystal tried to concentrate on reading the newspaper – more bad news everywhere, the economy in danger again, murderous militants roaming the Middle East, more MPs caught with their pants down… "You're very noisy today, Perkins. Put a sock in it." Crystal walked into the room where she had left him.

Perkins was still on the window sill looking out, and in a semi-circle on the grass stood at least twenty large crows, their raven-black feathers glistening bright in the sunlight. "This is weird. Is this your adopted family come to visit?" asked Crystal. "Hold it there, Perkins. I have to take a picture of this. Otherwise, David won't believe it when I tell him."

Crystal scurried upstairs and rummaged in the dressing table for her digital camera. *Hope the battery's charged*, she thought, pushing the on button. The lens slid out and the display lit up. *Great*, she thought, turning, only to see a cloud of black wings as the crows took flight and were soon lost among the trees along the front of the lake. "Bugger – you could have kept them talking a few minutes longer, Perkins," Crystal remarked, returning the camera to its drawer.

In bed that evening, she recounted the strange occurrence to David. "It's called a murder of crows – no idea why," he explained. "Might just have been a coincidence. They are intelligent and curious birds and probably heard Perkins and came over to investigate – bloody nuisance to farmers with crops though. They can strip a field bare, given half a chance. We're not even supposed to shoot them – go out and wave our hands and shout 'Shoo' according to the Min of Ag— "

"Yes, anyway, they seem to have given Perkins a home when he needed one, so I suppose I'm grateful to them – they must have some saving graces," said Crystal.

"Suppose they also grub out lots of pests," admitted David grudgingly. "Never going to love them, mind. Anyway, to change the subject, I was thinking the other day that it's nearly a year since you arrived in Bala, and bought the cottage. Are you going to have some sort of celebration?"

"I'd not really thought about it. I suppose I could have some sort of party – maybe a barbecue – invite all the people who've helped me since I arrived."

"Talking about old crows, I take it that won't be including Megan and her little group, the Women of the Mountains?" said David.

"No, or your old pal, Madog. I can still just about see some of the bruises he left you with – including to your ego when he knocked you out cold."

"Bugger got me when my back was turned. I had him on the ropes before then. I'd beat him any day in a fair fight, big as he is."

"If you say so, David. Anyway, I'll draw up a list of people and set a date, maybe in a couple of weeks. How would that fit in with you?"

"Sounds OK. I've a pal who does hog roasts at the local markets. We could get that set up along with the barbecue. A proper meat fest."

"Carnivore." Crystal punched him playfully in the stomach. "Not everyone wants great lumps of meat with everything. We'll also have some nice vegetarian options – Greek mezze, falafel and hummus – that sort of thing. I do a mean feta cheese and filo parcel, and how about some courgette fritters?"

"Can't wait," said David. "Go nicely with the lamb kebabs and Mr Jones' special bratwurst sausage and ribs extravaganza."

"Peasant. Go to sleep. And try not to wake me with your snoring tonight," Crystal turned out the light.

There was a moment of silence in the dark. "Is that it then? It's only just past eleven o'clock."

"Well, David. I'm open to suggestions."

* * *

Over the coming week Crystal sent out party invitations to everyone she could think of. There was Taff, landlord of the Glyndwr Arms, and the old naturist couple who she thought looked like two wrinkly Shar Peis when she painted them shortly before Christmas. They'd brought her in quite a lot of work from the rest of the naturist community in Wales, she reflected, so she'd better ask them. She just hoped they would arrive clothed – and had made sure the invitation included 'Dress Code Smart Casual' underlined. Freddie and Nigel had already booked the spare room, and Sylvie had promised to bring a quiche made with eggs from her own chickens.

David had invited lots of his friends from the local farming community. "It's going to be a great party, Ben. What do you think?" Ben just wagged his tail, and gave her a doggy smile. "During the party you can play with Skippy in the field, so you won't be underfoot. How would you like that?" At the mention of Skippy's name Ben padded to the door and barked, looking appealingly in Crystal's direction. "Not right now, Ben. Skippy is busy right now doing what men sheep do, and helping to make babies."

The first lambs were already in the field and Crystal could see that many of the sheep were fat with as yet unborn lambs. More sheep had been put in the field, and Skippy had buckled down, and was steadily working his way through the new flock.

She noticed that there were more crows in the surrounding trees of late, but put it down to the large number of sheep in the field, and the arrival of lambs. Hoping for a free meal, if one or two of them are stillborn, she presumed. She thought it made the cottage look quite gothic – very Edgar Allan Poe – with the large black birds sitting in the trees outside and pecking round the bird table. There had been no repeat of the strange gathering of crows outside the window, but Perkins still seemed restless, and sometimes pecked at the window as if wanting to be outside again. "I'd let you out, but you know what happened before," said Crystal. "I just can't risk it, and my doggy parrot whisperer may not be able to save you a second time. That's if he wants to – you ignore him most of the time."

That evening she decided on an early night, but in the small hours was woken from her sleep by Ben licking her face. "What's happening, Ben? You know you aren't allowed upstairs." She looked at her bedside clock. "It's after four in the morning, for God's sake."

Ben ran to the window and poked his head under the curtain to look out. Crystal joined him. "What's all the fuss? There's nothing out there."

Then she noticed a light moving in the field, and when she opened the window an inch or two could make out muffled voices. She saw what looked like a horsebox parked in the lane which led to the field, and to her driveway. As her eyes became accustomed to the dark, she made out three men, and what looked like a large, very scruffy, sheepdog, who were herding sheep towards the vehicle. "My God. Ben, we've got rustlers stealing the sheep. I must ring David. He'll know what to do."

Crystal picked up the phone and dialled David's number, which rang and rang for several minutes. "Come on, David. Pick up the damn phone," pleaded Crystal, before a very sleepy sounding voice came on the line. "Hi. What's up?"

Crystal quickly recounted what was happening in the field. "What should I do?"

"Nothing," said David, his voice sounding fully awake now. "Stay indoors and make sure you're all locked up. Some of these characters can be pretty violent. We have a contingency plan for this sort of thing. I'm going off the phone now, to call the police and round up the troops. We'll be over very soon. Just stay quiet, and keep your lights off. Don't do anything to draw attention to yourself."

Crystal peered out through the curtain again, and saw that most of the sheep were now in the horsebox. "Hurry up, David, or you'll miss them," she pleaded. Then she saw that two of the men had cornered Skippy, backing him up against the wire fence. One had hold of him by the horns and another had grabbed his tail and a hank of his long shaggy hair. Skippy was struggling as the men inched him toward the horsebox, but the sheepdog was nipping at his heels and the two men had him firmly in their grip. "He's a strong bugger yon tup," she heard, recognising from her youth a strong Cumbrian accent. She had spent many rainy summers on campsites up and down the Lake District, with her mum and dad, and knew it well.

"Right, that's it," announced Crystal. "No one messes with my Skippy – and anyway David'll be here in a minute or two with back-up."

She ran downstairs and out of the back door. "Hey, you there," she shouted. "What the bloody hell do you think you're doing – let go of my ram."

Ben came bounding past her out of the house, and jumped the wire fence, running straight at the sheepdog that was harrying Skippy, snarling as the two dogs collided, rolling over in a tangle of teeth and claws. Skippy renewed his struggle, but couldn't break free from the two men.

Crystal noticed a flash of feathers behind her, and saw Perkins fly through the door and into the trees outside, where he emitted a series of loud crow-like screeches. Bugger. This no longer seemed like such a good idea. One of the men turned and ran up the drive towards her, and in alarm she realised she didn't have time to get back through the door and lock it before he reached her. Ben had put up a fight, but the heavier dog was getting the better of him, and had him pinned on his back. No help coming from there.

It flashed into Crystal's mind that she was standing in her Beauty and the Beast jim jams and slippers and she felt exposed and vulnerable: "Come on David. Now would be a very good time to turn up." The man reached her, and she aimed her best punch at his head. It was like hitting a brick wall, and she felt rough hands grab her and bodily lift her up, pinioning her arms in a crushing bear hug. She felt sour breath on her face. "Still got something to say, lass? Maybe me and the lads have just got a bonus – a bit of sauce to go with t'lamb before we leave."

"Let go you sheep-shagging bastard." Crystal twisted and turned to try and bite the man's face.

He laughed coarsely. "Hey lads, look what we've got here – a right little minx, and all alone by the looks of it."

Crystal heard Perkins squawking in the trees, and saw crows gathering from the surrounding woodland, forming into a huge spiral that swirled high into the sky. The plume of black feathers coiled upwards, more birds joining the massive flock as it spiralled, then turned and swooped toward the field, led by a huge crow with a long murderous-looking beak. The noise they were making was deafening – a pre-dawn chorus from hell.

The men holding Skippy were the first to face the murder of crows, as they attacked. The birds pecked furiously at their faces and claws attached to bodies, long beaks inflicting damage. The men tried to swat away their attackers, but in vain as more joined in the battle.

The sheepdog fared even worse – his whole body at the mercy of the crows. They formed a moving black mass on his fur, and the large crow was pecking at his eyes. The dog struggled, howling in agony, but it was useless and soon his paws gave way and he collapsed onto the grass. His struggles ceased and he stopped moving – carrion for the crows to feast on.

Skippy and Ben were free and ran toward the fence. Ben cleared it first, closely followed by Skippy, and closed fast on the man holding Crystal. He tried to run, but by now Ben had his trousers in his teeth and was tugging him back as the much heavier Skippy ran at him full tilt, knocking him off his feet. The crows joined in the attack, and the man staggered to his feet and ran towards the horsebox, batting away crows as he went and with Ben still snapping at his heels.

Crystal heard the sound of sirens and saw flashing blue lights heading fast across the causeway. The rustlers made it back to the horsebox, and she heard the engine start up. But before it could move she saw David's Ford pick-up slide to a stop, blocking their exit. Behind him an array of pick-ups and Range Rovers pulled in, and a group of burly farmers leapt out, including Ted, whose sheep were about to be rustled, carrying what looked to her like a pickaxe handle.

Sensibly, the would-be thieves decided to wait in the horsebox until the police arrived moments later.

Perkins flew down from his treetop eyrie and landed on Crystal's shoulder. "Well done, Perkins. But I do look a bit like the pirate lady with you perched there. Pieces of eight eh?"

"Pieces of eight," repeated Perkins, before fluttering back inside, to settle on his perch.

Crystal watched as the men were handcuffed and led away. "She's a fuckin' witch yonder one," said her attacker as a policeman dragged him protesting towards a patrol car. "Them birds killed our dog, and tried bloody hard to have us. We've 'ad buggery pecked out on us. It should be her you're arresting for grievous bodily harm. She controls t'animals, and they do what she says."

"Nothing to do with me, actually. It was all down to my friends." Crystal patted Ben's head and he padded inside. "I think you'll find that they acted of their own accord – I never asked them to do anything. Matter of fact you assaulted me, you – what was it I called you? Oh yes. Sheep-shagging bastard. See you in court."

David ran to her side. "You OK? What happened to waiting inside until we arrived?"

"You took your time. I couldn't let them steal Skippy, could I?" said Crystal. "And it seems I've had a bit of help from the animal kingdom, thanks to Perkins who seems to have rallied the avian troops to our side. And very effective they were."

She looked across at where a group of crows were still pecking at the remains of the sheepdog. "Pity about the dog. Don't suppose it was his fault his masters were criminals."

"The crows are just claiming what's due," said David. "It'll be nothing but a carcass in an hour or two. I've had a word with the police, and they want you to go to the station tomorrow, and make a full statement. It's not far from daylight." David looked to where a faint glimmer of light could be seen in the sky to the east.

Crystal shivered, suddenly remembering she was stood in her jim jams and slippers. "Better go inside. Fancy a cuppa?"

* * *

The next day, as Crystal got ready to go to the police station, the phone rang. "Hello. It's Ted here. Just to thank you for last night. Not sure what happened with the bird thing, but a lot of people round here are already saying you have special powers – they can be a superstitious lot, you know, so expect a few funny looks. I've been a farmer for nigh on thirty years, and never seen the like.

"Anyway, you saved me quite a bit of money. It's expensive to insure against stuff like that, and to be honest I hadn't bothered. The stress means some of the sheep will probably abort their lambs, but it would have been a lot worse if they'd got away with it, so thanks. You'll not be going short of lamb this winter."

"Thanks, Ted. Matter of fact, I'm about to go to the police station to give them a statement. I don't know myself how to explain the birds, except to say it was Perkins that called for his friends, and they came. Have you heard anything more from the police about who those men were? Not from anywhere round here, that's for sure."

"Police told me they're from up round Carlisle way. The one who grabbed you was the ringleader – has previous convictions for poaching wild deer, sheep rustling and a string of assaults – a real bad'n. The others were part of his extended family. Bunch of layabouts apparently. He'll be going down for quite a while I imagine, as he's got previous convictions and was out on licence from a previous prison sentence. Pity they don't still hang the buggers or transport them somewhere very unpleasant. That's my view."

"They'll certainly be doing some bird, if you get my meaning. Anyway, got to go Ted. See you soon." Crystal hung up the phone.

Later that day, she gave her statement to a young constable at the police station in Dolgellau. She wasn't sure he believed her about the birds, because at this point in her story he licked his pencil and looked confused: "Are you sure that's what happened? It was quite dark at the time, and I wouldn't like to say what a jury is going to make of it all."

But Crystal stuck by her account, and eventually it was all down on paper. She signed the statement, thanked the young copper for his patience, and left.

She returned to Bala to wander round the shops for a while before going home, and noticed that Ted was right. People looked at her, and openly gossiped together as she passed by. News got around pretty quickly here, she knew, and realised she was fast becoming the barking mad birdwoman of Bala – with a menagerie of talking animals at her command. All she needed now was to be seen shopping on a Segway, with Perkins perched on her shoulder and Ben loping at her side, to complete the madcap image.

Mad, but popular, she soon found. She returned home to see on her emails that Ted had nominated her as National Farmers' Union Woman of the Month, for foiling the rustlers, and her Facebook page was full of praise for standing up to them. Should be Perkins getting all the plaudits she supposed, but didn't mind bathing in the reflected glory for a while.

One of the posts was from poet and recent friend Gruff Griff: "Hello, Crystal love. Once again you have inspired me to write a little limerick, which goes as follows:

> *I once knew an artist called Crystal*
> *An epic force that blows like the Mistral.*
> *She talks to the crows*
> *In both blank verse and prose*
> *And has breasts that remind me of Bristol.*

Sorry, couldn't resist. When are you going to dump that farm boy, and go out with a real man? That would be me, by the way.
All the best,
Your biggest fan, Gruff the ever hopeful."

Crystal smiled: *Daft bugger*. She thought for a minute or two, and typed her reply:

> "*I once knew a poet called Gruff*
> *Always on the lookout for a bit of rough*
> *He asked out a lass*
> *But she was out of his class*
> *So sorry old lad, but tough.*

PS: Hope you can make my party this weekend. Everyone but Megan invited."

***

Crystal spent the next morning fending off calls from newspapers, even some national dailies, but told them all that the police had asked her not to say anything, as the three men involved had all been charged with sheep rustling. "They told me it's bona fides or something – no, sub judice. That's the phrase they used. It means I can't say anything until after the court case. Thanks anyway," she said putting the phone down on the latest caller.

Almost immediately the phone rang again: "Hello, it's Sally Evans from Radio Free Gwynedd. I see you're in the news again – strange story about birds attacking sheep rustlers. You don't do things normal, do you? I wondered if you might like to appear on the programme – we could get an ornithologist on as well, and a few local farmers, to talk us through what happened— "

"Sorry, Sally. It's all been blown a little out of proportion, and you remember what happened last time I appeared on your show. I ended up on the wrong side of Megan and her bunch of loonies from Women of the Mountains, so I'd have to think about it."
Then say no, she thought.

"Any case, I can't say anything until they've been tried, and hopefully convicted. The police tell me it could take months before it gets to court. Meanwhile they're safely banged up somewhere – Liverpool I think. Why not come to my party, though? I've been here for almost a year, and I'm planning a bit of a celebration – you could bring along that receptionist you have there – the one with all the make-up."

"She's not with us anymore. Got a better paid job on the tills, down at the local Co-op. We've a lovely new front-of-house person. Very jolly, but does tend to pick her nose in front of visitors and never flushes the chain when she goes to the lavvy. Probably doesn't wash her hands either. I make my own tea now, mind. Send me an invitation, and if I can I'll come over."

Crystal put the phone down. Afternoon already – and she hadn't felt the sun on her face once that day. Everyone had now been invited to the party, and most were coming. She hadn't heard from Old Huw yet, which was unusual, since he rarely turned down the chance of a free drink and food. *He'll probably just turn up,* she thought. "Come on, Ben. Walkies. Perkins," she shouted. "Guard the house. We'll be back in an hour."

* * *

The day of the party dawned, and Crystal had gathered a small army of friends to help her. David had been packed off down to Mr Jones to pick up the meat for his carnivores' banquet, and he already had the half-barrel BBQ primed and ready to go. The hog roast had arrived at first light, and was already giving off delicious meaty smells, as a whole hog slowly roasted in its own juices.

Crystal and Sylvie were up to their armpits in salads, dips and pastry, and the fridge was packed with bottles of wine and beer, provided by Taff from the Glyndwr Arms at a discount price. The sun was shining, and it looked like a perfect day – a cloudless sky over Lake Bala, where kayaks slowly paddled past, and a dinghy made little progress in the light breeze. Ben was already sitting on the grass next to Skippy, soaking up the late summer sun, and lambs bleated and followed their mothers round the field.

"People will be arriving in less than an hour," said Crystal. "Can you hold the fort, Sylvie, while I go and have a shower and get changed? You've got flour all over your face by the way."

Sylvie turned. "I know. I'm a messy cook. Go and have your shower, and if it's OK I'll nip in and freshen up when you've finished."

"I'll be ten minutes. Promise," said Crystal. "Lucky I don't spend hours on make-up. The two Fs, a bit of lippy, and I'm done."

Crystal had just stepped out of the shower when she heard a loud screech, and a bellow of laughter. She smiled. Freddie had arrived. The noise level would soon hit decibel-splitting level, and the fridge space for booze would be even more challenged. Freddie's husband Nigel always brought a huge collection of assorted bottles of wine with him to parties. She quickly towelled off, slipped into jeans and her favourite kaftan and went downstairs. "All yours Sylvie, but you might want to give it a few minutes, if you know what I mean? Only joking. It's fine."

Several people had arrived while she had been in the shower, Gruff was chatting to Nigel, both with large glasses of white wine in their hands. "Hi guys. See you found the largest glasses – they're really for beer you know."

"Hello, Crystal, how are you?" said Gruff. "Big glasses – less filling up. Saves time, you see."

David had arrived back from the butcher and was busy firing up a second barbecue. Farmer Ted – resplendent in new red overalls that in his world passed for smart casual – was helping him. "I've seen less smoke coming from the steam train," shouted Crystal, as David glanced across and waved through the smoke.

"It'll be fine once it dies down a bit." David coughed and mopped watery eyes with a tissue, as Ted tipped yet more charcoal onto the flames.

An hour into the party, and Crystal cast a satisfied glance round her assembled guests – everything was pretty well going to plan. Freddie had already fallen over once, and spilled a whole glass of red wine over Ted's best overalls, followed by a glass of white wine she chucked over him, declaring it would stop the red wine staining his rural chic attire.

Thoroughly drenched, Ted was now wearing Crystal's pink jogging pants, and an oversized bright green T-shirt she had bought at a jumble sale because she felt sorry for the glum-faced old biddy who had it on her stall. She smiled at the thought of Ted going home in his new wardrobe, and explaining to his wife why he was dressed like that. His wife never went to parties, and Crystal thought she always had a rather sour look on her face. Ted told her it was because they had never had children. "Something to do with the sheep dip we used to use shrinking the old testicles, so the doctor said," Ted explained. "Personally, I think it's because she weighs at least twenty stone, and I can't get near, if you know what I mean. Like trying to make love to a huge bouncy castle and just prodding in the general direction, in the hope you're on target."

"Thanks Ted. I'll probably have to live with that vision for the rest of my life," said Crystal, moving swiftly away to talk to other guests.

Nigel and Gruff had moved on to vodka slammers, and were matching each other pretty equally, and David was busy serving his meat mountain to a long line of locals. Crystal noted that the guacamole and hummus dips didn't seem to be going down quite as well – untouched in fact. "Peasants," she muttered under her breath, and took another gulp of Aldi's best Chianti. Still no Huw or his son Gwyndaf though. Strange. She felt a cloud pass overhead, blocking the sun, and shivered. *I'll give him a ring tomorrow*, she promised herself. For now, there was serious drinking to do.

* * *

As the sun began to set on the lake, casting long shadows across the lawn, people began to drift off. Nigel and Gruff had retreated to a corner and were now sipping beer, their laughter subdued. Crystal realised Gruff wasn't going anywhere tonight - wasn't sure he could even stand – and had already sorted out an old sleeping bag for him. "Worst comes to the worst, we'll just have to open up the bag and chuck it over both of them. It's a warm night so they should be OK out here," she told David, who had come to join her on the swinging seat near the kitchen door.

Freddie was already inside, on the sofa snoring loudly.

Sylvie had said her goodbyes, and had retreated with her husband back up the hill to the farmhouse, turning down an offer of a taxi. "Walk will do us good. I'll come down some time tomorrow to give you a hand clearing up." She donned a sturdy set of walking shoes, and produced a torch from her handbag. "See you later – and thanks. Wonderful party."

"Thank you," Crystal replied. "I couldn't have got everything done without you."

David was finishing his beer – still surprisingly sober. *Too busy serving food to get drunk*, she presumed – *or maybe saving himself for me.* "Good party," he said. "I thought it went well, but Huw never turned up. It's unusual for him not to even give an explanation."

"I'll ring tomorrow and find out," said Crystal. "He was looking a bit peaky and sounded a bit chesty last time I saw him – but I've never known him turn down a free drink. Maybe he just got a better offer." She still found Huw's non-appearance worrying, and it kept her awake during the night – she didn't know why it troubled her, but she just felt something must be wrong. Up at first light, she made herself a cup of tea, ignoring the symphony of snoring from the house guests who hadn't managed to make it home.

"I'll have a cup if you're making it," came a voice from the back room, as Gruff emerged, fully dressed. His long, greying hair was out of the usual ponytail and looked like it had been hit by a minor hurricane.

"How are you feeling after yesterday? You and Nigel were certainly knocking it back."

"Water off a duck's back, love. A bit of a drink helps keep the artistic juices flowing, don't you think? Not sure about Nigel though. Looked a bit tipsy last I saw him. I hope you don't have wardrobes in the bedroom he was in – the state he was in, he didn't seem to quite understand the concept of using the toilet. Last I saw he was outside pissing in a flower pot."

Bugger. There goes the alchemilla mollis again, thought Crystal. "If I'd had as much as you it wouldn't be artistic juices flowing. I'd have spent half the night speaking to God on the big white telephone," she said, making a mental note to investigate the wardrobe full of her best clothes as soon as Nigel and Freddie had left. "Anyway, I'm glad you enjoyed yourself and managed not to assault any of my guests." She placed a cup of tea on the counter in front of Gruff.

Ben had appeared at her side, and looked appealingly into her eyes. "What do you want?" Crystal asked. "Surely you don't want feeding at this time in the morning?"

The dog continued staring Crystal out. "Come on then – but no more until lunchtime. OK?"

Crystal fed Ben, and glanced at the clock on the wall. Probably all right to phone Huw now – it was past 8am, and folk tended to get up early in the country, she had found. The dawn chorus often woke her up now, particularly since Perkins had taken to joining in with his friends outside.

She dialled Huw's number and waited for a full minute before the phone was lifted, and answered by Huw's son Gwyndaf: "Hello Gwyndaf. Is the old bugger around – he was supposed to be coming to my party yesterday, but never turned up. Same goes for you."

There was a long pause on the line. "You haven't heard then," said Gwyndaf, his voice breaking as he spoke. "There's no easy way of saying this, but my dad passed away last night."

Crystal's mouth felt dry, and she felt her hand trembling. "I'm so sorry, Gwyndaf," she said, her own voice cracking-up. *What else to say?* She felt hot tears on her face, and wiped them away with her hand.

"Bronchitis it was," said Gwyndaf. "He seemed to be getting better, but then suddenly took a turn for the worse – turned into pneumonia, the doctor said. He was taken by ambulance to Glan Clwyd Hospital, but fell into a coma, and the doctors couldn't save him. I thought he'd put up more of a fight, but in the end he just slipped away like he knew his time had come."

Crystal heard herself asking about funeral arrangements, and whether there was anything she could do – detached like she was in another room – and heard Gwyndaf tell her he'd be in touch as soon as he knew.

She put the phone down, as Gruff walked back into the room. "Any chance of a bit of toast to go with the— what's wrong Crystal love? You're white as a sheet."

Crystal turned to the poet and tried to speak – but no words came. She heard him shout for David and heard steps on the stairs…

* * *

A joker to the end, Huw's last will and testament stipulated that his body lie in state for an evening at the Glyndwr Arms before a service and burial at the local Anglican church the next day, and he had made provision to leave £200 behind the bar to give him a rousing send-off. "First time he's stood a round that I remember," Taff, the landlord, told Crystal, when she called to ask what arrangements had been made. "Still, better late than never, I suppose, though 200 quid's not going to go very far. I expect half of Bala's going to turn up, whether it's to toast Huw's passing, or just for a free drink on the old bugger. Suppose I can stand a few pints on the house myself, and a hotpot supper for those able to eat it," he offered.

There was consternation at the local funeral director's office, who were tasked with giving Huw a decent burial, and at the brewery who questioned whether the pub's licence extended to hosting dead bodies. But Taff argued that it was right and proper Huw be given a proper send-off of his own choosing, and the brewery reluctantly acceded the point after reviewing the lease and concluding there were no exclusion clauses that specifically banned a person from one of their pubs just because they happened to be dead. "He spent half his life here, so I don't see why we shouldn't send him off with a toast of a pint of Brains best bitter," said Taff.

The pub was closed for normal business for the evening, but the invited guest list meant it was pretty much like a normal busy night, apart from the coffin propped up on chairs. Crystal and David had arrived early, and Taff solemnly poured them a couple of pints. "Here's to Old Huw. May he rest in peace." Taff raised his own glass and took a deep swig.

"Not sure they're ready for him, wherever he's going," said Crystal as she and David also raised their glasses. It struck her that Huw looked strangely peaceful in his open coffin, like he was about to wake up and order a pint.

"I noticed you've taken down the picture I painted," said Crystal, glancing behind the bar to where it usually hung.

"Yes. Hope you don't mind. It didn't seem right somehow," said Taff. "Anyhow, it's sort of going with him." He glanced toward where Huw lay.

"You haven't?" Crystal gazed aghast at the coffin.

"Well, you always said he had a sense of humour, so I just sort of tucked it down the side. He's only a small bloke so there was plenty of room. Thought it would be a fitting send-off. He never took himself too serious, after all, but I can get it back if you want. Just need to move him to one side a bit if you could give me a hand." Taff rounded the bar and headed towards the coffin.

"No you're all right," said Crystal hurriedly. "Let's just leave him and the picture where they are."

The pub was soon crammed with well-wishers and hangers-on, and Taff replaced the coffin lid, and put a Welsh flag over it after he heard one bunch of slightly rowdy locals suggest getting Old Huw out for one last drink at the White Lion down the road. He decided that would be a joke too far.

By 10pm Huw's coffin sat in a corner, more or less forgotten, except a few locals were using it as a handy table for their pints as they stood and swapped memories of the cantankerous old geezer. *Amazing how soon the coffin became just another piece of furniture*, thought Crystal. *Would anyone notice if we just left it there? Could be the first pub in Wales with a sarcophagus.*

She and David downed another couple of pints, and decided to call it a night. "See you tomorrow at the funeral, Taff," she shouted, as they headed for the door.

He looked up from the taps, where he was busy pulling pints, and nodded farewell.

* * *

Crystal and David waited for the funeral cortège to draw up outside the church. The summer sun shone bright in their eyes, and Crystal noticed many of their fellow mourners were looking a bit worse for wear. Some had sunglasses on and others were squinting badly, and holding their heads. Conversation was muted. She had been asked by Huw's son, Gwyndaf, to say a few words during the service, as she had been one of his best friends in the final months of his life, and she fingered her crib notes nervously. She had never been any good at public speaking, even at school.

David held her hand, as the black hearse drew up, followed by two stretch limousines. Gwyndaf stepped out of the leading car, and nodded briefly in Crystal's direction as the coffin was taken out, and he and three other bearers lifted it onto their shoulders and carried it into church to a recording of Charlotte Church singing 'Ave Maria', one of Huw's favourite songs. Another was 'The Birdie Song', which Gwyndaf had decreed would finish the service.

The vicar began with a eulogy of Huw's life, which showed he obviously didn't know the man at all. Crystal couldn't blame him – the only times Huw had set foot in the church in the last half century had been for his wedding, and many years later the funeral of his wife.

Gwyndaf sat with his head bowed, surrounded by other family members, as the service continued, and the vicar nodded to Crystal. "If Crystal would step forward, I believe she has a short eulogy to Huw." He glanced nervously at his watch. Another funeral party were already waiting in the drive to the church.

Crystal took to the lectern: "Hello everybody, and on behalf of Huw's family I'd like to thank you all for turning out in such numbers. As you probably all know, Huw and I didn't have the best of starts, and for quite a time I suppose you could say we weren't the best of friends.

"But we got over that, and when I got to know Huw better, I came to appreciate his finer points. He had a wicked sense of humour. I don't think anyone would say he was perfect – far from it. But who is? And Huw was… how can I say it?… a one-off. There was no one else like him. He was funny, kind to his friends once you got to know him, and had a unique outlook on life, even if people sometimes got a little rubbed up the wrong way by his sense of humour. I know I did, and I'm pretty sure Gwyndaf didn't really like being called Gandalf for half his adult life. But for all his faults, maybe partly because of them, we all loved Huw for his personality, flaws and all.

"Most of us get our individuality chiselled off over the years. We become a bit homogenous – all a bit the same. That never happened to Huw. Take it or leave it he was his own man – and one we will all really miss. I'll finish now, but thank you for listening." Crystal stepped down and resumed her seat.

There followed a recital of 'Keep Right On To The End Of The Road' in Welsh by Gwyndaf –and by now the vicar was looking seriously concerned. He continually glanced at his watch and fingered his dog collar – his Adam's apple bouncing up and down under the stiff fabric, like it was tied to an elastic band, every time he swallowed. Then it was over, and they all filed out of the church to the strains of 'The Birdie Song'.

Crystal and David had decided not to intrude on the graveside ceremony, deciding it should be for a private affair for the family, but Gwyndaf hurried after them: "Thank you for the words. It summed him up pretty well I thought. Before they took him to hospital he asked me to give you this – said you would appreciate it." He produced the twisted old stick that Huw had used for his impersonation of Harry Lauder.

"Thank you, Gwyndaf," said Crystal. "I'll treasure it."

"That'll come in useful," said David, as they walked from the church.

"I know, but what could I say? Maybe I'll give it to Ben – he likes a good chew."

*　*　*

The stick lay in the corner of Crystal's living room. She hadn't given it to Ben, and supposed she would have to keep it somewhere, or find a use for it.

Perkins had been unusually quiet. She wondered if he missed Huw, who had always talked at length to the bird whenever he visited. Crystal also missed the frequent knock at the door – Huw standing there asking if there was any chance of a cup of tea and a piece of bara brith. The stick had given her an idea, however, and soon she was hard at work. Paint flew onto the canvas, and once again Huw slowly came back to life – not nude this time, but dressed as Harry Lauder. Crystal closed her eyes and pictured him – the tatty old kilt hanging down to his ankles, the old stick, but most of all the wicked glint in his eyes, which seemed to follow her round the room, and the wily smile. But something else –a love of life that lurked in his face. When the painting was finally complete, Crystal stepped back with a satisfied smile.

Taff had been right – the original painting of Huw would no longer have been appropriate – but Crystal felt sure she had now captured the essential character of the man – possibly the best painting she had ever done.

She glanced out of the window, a tear in her eye, and noticed that Ted had given the sheep in the field their summer shearing, including Skippy, who had lost his trademark dreadlocks and she thought looked rather handsome with his short back and sides. The trim accentuated his manly attributes which had been masked by his shaggy fleece even though they hung remarkably low. Then she noticed that Ted, when he had re-marked the sheep with dye, had also painted a big letter C on all of them. Skippy also had a large C sprayed on, but with a rough crown painted on the top of it. *Daft bugger, Ted,* she thought. *Fitting though – a year in Wales and now I have a flock of sheep named after me. I've arrived.*